Balance of Power in Shepherds Pass

Alex Mitchell

Published by Alex Mitchell, 2023.

BALANCE OF POWER IN SHEPHERDS PASS

First edition. November 17, 2023.

ISBN: 979-8891980228

Written by Alex Mitchell.

Also by Alex Mitchell

BALANCE OF POWER IN SHEPHERDS PASS

Chapter 1

"Now that is what I call a cute couple," Abby commented to Lavon as they approached Wendell and Webber. Officer Webbers turned to face Abby. Webber is an athletically built woman in her early thirties. She is a police officer for the Shepherds Pass police department.

This evening, she wore a strapless almond dress that contoured and defined every segment of her body, if not highlighted them. Webber's physique gave tribute to every sit-up, push-up, and crunch Webber had endured to be in such magnificent shape. Her short hair had been professionally tended, and Webber's wife had masterfully applied Webber's makeup; now, only the deadly stare she imposed in Abby's direction blemished her face artistically.

Shepherds Pass is a small Missouri town that grew out of a truck stop repair shop and then the illegal operations of two brothers, Leo, and Raymond Dodd. Leo would spend the latter years of his life fighting to legitimize the small town. At the same time, his brother Raymond enveloped himself in organized crime. In the late 1950s, the highway rerouting project had been completed, which now represents what we know as Highway 70. This highway was part of the dream of US politicians to connect both ends of the US through a highway system. The completion of this project meant that travelers no longer had to exit the highway and find a new road somewhere else to cross the country. The new highway structure also meant that the small town of Shepherds Pass was now booming from the spillover effect.

On this evening in 2023, celebrating something much less political, or at least for appearance's sake, was underway. Like many small growing towns with no National sports teams, Shepherds Pass spent great fanfare celebrating its local nonprofessional sports persons. The great hope was that if stars in sport bloomed for Shepherds Pass someday, it would catch the eye of the pro sports world.

Lavon Tyler and Addy Blackwell are Shepherds Pass Detectives. A large group had gathered in the Leo Dodd Community Center to present an award to many exceptional young athletes. Since a large group of politicians and news people from outside Shepherds Pass had been invited to watch the presentation, lured by a free meal, Shepherds Pass police provided security.

"You can unload those eyeballs, young lady," Lavon noticed the glare coming from Webber, "Abby and I were noticing how, since we have a shortage of detectives and had to put uniformed cops in semi-formal wear for the shindig. So many of our guys stand out like a sore thumb."

"What do you expect? Most of these jokers don't have a clue what they should be wearing." Wendell responded. Wendell was a Police Sergeant and a close friend of Lavon and Webbers. Wendell had recently been promoted to police Sargent. Wendell was thirty years old and smaller in frame than Lavon but had a strong boxer's body. Wendell had recently won the light heavy weight competition for charity against the fire department. He and Lavon had trained together to assure mutual victories. Wendell had deliberately chosen to ignore how Abby's comment that had scorched Webber.

"I am sorry, ma'am. I should learn not to be so touchy." Webber offered. Webber is married to a female firefighter in Shepherds Pass. In the past, Abby had vaulted homophobic slurs at Webber.

Currently, the small group had agreed on a truce, and in the interest of work, no one wanted to be the first to violate the peace accord.

"No sweat. How's the arm?" Abby could feel the group dynamic shifting back to her. Was everyone waiting for her to say something out of place and inappropriate? Webber had been shot twice recently in the line of duty, both in the left shoulder.

"The arm is fine. It got me a medal of valor and a citation of bravery in the line of fire." Webber answered, rubbing the bandage that was the one less fashionable addition to her ensemble. "If I keep hanging out with you guys, I will be either the most decorated female cop in Shepherds Pass history or dead."

This joke brought a needed relieving chuckle from the group as they paned the crowd.

"Love Bird at eleven o'clock." Abby broke the silence. Lynn Dodd-Masterson, Lavon's girlfriend, had entered view. She was on the left arm of Dolan Dodd, her uncle, and a reputed gangster.

There was a younger version of Lynn on Dolan's right arm. Both women wore matching tangerine dresses, and they set the attention of the room into the air like bottle rockets. There was a group of apparent bodyguards. Two of the bodyguards were blocking anyone approaching Dolan. There were two other bodyguards one male and one female: they had been assigned to protect JoAnn.

JoAnn was Dolans sister and confidant.

JoAnn entered wearing a robin's egg blue dress. JoAnn took the opportunity to wink at Lavon from across the room.

"Excuse me. Can I ask you a question?" A young woman, plainly one of the athletes being honored, had run up to Lavon in his moment of distraction. The woman looked to be a hair under twenty years old. Lavon was six foot two, but the young woman was much taller than him.

"How can we help you, honey?" Abby asked.

"You can't. I was talking to cutie pie here." Wendell cleared his throat to keep from laughing as Webber muffled a chuckle. "Someone told me you are related to S. Rowen Tyler. The writer."

Lavon looked up at the tall, slender, muscular black girl, unsure where this was going.

"That's the rumor going around my house. Has been for quite some time." Lavon did not attempt to mask his Southern accent.

"Give him this," the young woman shoved an envelope in Lavon's hand. "Tell him my name is Jackie Bones Jones, and I am going to be a superstar in the WMBA. And I would do anything to spend the evening with him. And I do mean anything. That man knows how to write what is in a woman's soul."

It took a moment for Webber, Wendell, and Abby to regain their composure. By this time, Lavon was staring at the Lynn doppelganger as she stared back at him.

"So, I have an idea. Suppose you were considering getting your father a tie for Father's Day. I say cancel that. Get him the gift that he plans to keep on giving." This comment caused Webber, who had begun to regain her resolve, to lose it all over again.

"I can see it now; look what I brought you, Dad. A giant woman." Abby jested, trying to impersonate Lavon's accent.

"Who's the young girl with Dolan?" Lavon asked.

The group stopped laughing and stared at Lavon as if he had asked the dumbest question imaginable.

"Don't mind my partner, guys. He failed Shepherd Pass history." Abby tried to explain.

"That is Miss Paden Dodd. And if she looks familiar, it is because you most likely have seen her on TV. She was part of the pro tennis circuit." Webber tried to help.

Lavon still looked confused—something needed to be added to the explanation he had just received.

Wendell read the confused look and rushed to the rescue. "She is Dolan Dodd's granddaughter."

Lavon had a question, but it was shoved to the back of his mind. There was something wrong in this room, and a clock was ticking on his, figuring out what it was. Cop instincts had catapulted forward in his mind. The tall basketball-playing girl had accosted Dolan's Granddaughter, no doubt for an autograph. Dolan formed the closet thing a tough gangster could to a smile and started walking toward the stage. Wait, Lavon thought. That waiter ignored that elderly woman trying to get him to pour her water from a pitcher he held. Lavon followed the servers' eyes and saw another waiter who looked almost exactly like the first.

The two waiters exchanged glances and smiled.

The first waiter's eyes shifted to something in the crowd. Not something you idiot, Lavon's brain commanded. Someone.

The waiter had a bald spot and thinning hair, but his mid-section was round. Just as Lavon was on his final collecting of clues, the first waiter pulled out an automatic handgun. The pistol slowly lowered toward its intended target.

Dolan turned slightly and almost acknowledged the death racing toward him at over one thousand feet per second. There were two pops. The first waiter staggered back. Lavon had landed two shots center mass into the waiter's midsection. The look of anger overtook any pain the waiter may have felt. Lavon thought body armor, that's the part of what I am seeing that was missing, and Lavon corrected his mistake by firing two shots into the forehead of the waiter.

The crowd went wild. People were screaming and shouting. Through the monolith of hysteria, Lavon heard his name called. It was Lynn rushing through the crowed to grab him.

"Sorry, Judge, his ass is all mine right now." Abby had reached Lynn and blocked her before Lynn could get to Lavon.

Lavon looked up, and Webber and Wendell appeared as though part of a magic act. Wendell and Webber now both wore their game faces.

"Wendell, get your guys to get everyone out of here and onto the parking lot. No one leaves until Lieutenant Nash says so. Webber, we got a second shooter.

He disappeared through the kitchen doors." Lavon barked out.

"I can back you up," Webber suggested.

"Negative, buddy. That is what she is here for." Lavon stated, looking at Abby. "We are going to send out the kitchen staff and keep them separated from the guests that were on the floor. Always keep them in front of you; we don't want any surprises."

"Did you have eyes on?" Abby asked, searching for the man who lay dead on the floor.

"Yeah, they look like brothers."

"This asshole is wearing ceramic body armor; we can assume his brother shops at the same bad guy store."

In a professional restaurant kitchen, there are usual entry doors and exit doors. People are only allowed to enter through the entry door and exit door only through exit doors. This is designed to keep servers from colliding with someone coming from the opposite direction when the load they are carrying is so great it obstructs their view. Lavon knew the only way the second waiter could have gotten past him was that he went in through an exit door. When Lavon and Abby entered the kitchen at first, they were hardly noticed. There was so much noise in the kitchen no one had heard the gunshots if they had gone off in the kitchen, let alone the next room. The kitchen was a beehive of activity. Salad prep people were making the salad in the hastiest and messiest way possible. Cooks were concocting God knows what and doing it in the loudest possible while trying to yell to each other over what looked like mass confusion.

"Alright, may I have your attention? "Abby shouted. Once the crowd noticed she and Lavon had guns pointed at them, they quickly complied. "Everybody freeze and stay exactly where you are. We are going to play a little game. Now I call this game, Abby says." The kitchen workers needed clarification. "You see, my name is Abby, and you play the game a lot, like Simon says. No one moves until I tell them. When I point to you, I want you to walk to the dining room floor and wait with the charming young lady there."

"Are we going to die?" A grey-haired older woman wearing an apron covered in so many unidentifiable sauces that looked like an abstract painting asked.

"Well, yes, but only if you don't play the game right. You see, whereas Simon has never shot anyone in the ass, Abby has." Abby responded.

"Abby, can we get on with this? You are having way too much fun." Lavon instructed.

Abby walked the room, selecting people that in no way fit the profile Lavon had given her but careful to keep the flow of people headed for the dining room slow and constant, not to overwhelm Webber waiting on the other side of the door.

Lavon saw something resembling a white cloth wad beneath a steel table. He reached down to pull the cloth out, and he felt the gentle tap of something on the back of his head. Bam. Bam. There were two shots. A warm, wet sprag covered the left side of Lavon's head. He reached to wipe it from his eyes. The warm spray had a gritty quality. A body slid down the wall and landed, facing Lavon. The second waiter's eyes were wide open, viewing death as it approached. Abby had shot the second waiter the second he got a good bead on Lavon. Lavon investigated the face of the dead and thought, go into shock later, for now finished the mission.

"Abby, let's keep clearing the room in case of a third shooter." Lavon managed to resolve to sound normal. "And Abby. Thank you."

A few minutes later."Auggh." Abby squealed.

"What?"

"This cake. The frosting is nothing but lard, food color, and powdered sugar. I say we find the chef and pop his ass."

Chapter 2

The following morning showed few signs that it would be fruitful for Lavon. At thirty-four, he was used to sleeping six hours or less. But it was almost early morning when he had finished questioning guests, workers, and general staff at the Dodd Center. The case had been assigned to Detective O'Leary, who disliked Lavon and Abby. Lavon's pretended to protest, but he was glad. Lavon and Lynn lived together with her maid in a stone semi-mansion. She was a Judge, and he was a Detective; they had an agreement. He did not have to discuss open cases with her for fear it would influence her decisions. In return, Lynn would recuse herself from cases involving him. This arrangement was stretched and tested as it was still in its infancy, but they had hope.

The second drawback to capturing sleep was that Lynn had left the crime scene before he did and had gone home to catch a sound night's sleep.

A sound sleep was utterly the opposite of what she received. Twice as Lavon had drifted off, he was awakened by Lynn having a nightmare. What is more, she refused to discuss what the nightmare was about. Lavon had tried to resign himself to the notion that the events of the evening had frightened a part of her, and she did not want to seem weak.

"YOU MUST BE DETECTIVE Tyler." A rail-thin black man in a three-piece suit had appeared unnoticed by Lavon or Abby. The detective squad room was new, as was the police station. The old building had a maze of desks in an open forum. The new squad room had two-person cubicles and plexiglass partitions to provide some noise-proofing for the occupants. It also meant that sometimes people showed up unseen until they were close.

Abby looked up to view the visitor and it was clear she knew him.

Lavon quickly shoved some pictures he had been viewing under a pile and offered his hand for a handshake.

"I am Detective Ivy. I will be handling the shooting review, among some other minor matters." Ivy smiled and revealed some gold teeth on the front right of this mouth. Ivy was dark, with even darker skin than Wendell, Lavon's friend.

"Be careful, Tyler. Detective Tyler not only works shooting reviews but also police intelligence. He is probably the one cop in Shepherds Pass who is almost as smart as you." Abby commented.

"Thank you, Abby. I will accept that as a backhand compliment." Ivy did not bother to release Lavon's hand. "And Detective Tyler, there is no need for subterfuge and hiding those stills, you were reviewing when I walked up."

"I was just."

And before Lavon could finish, Ivy filled in. "Those are pictures from the security cameras at last night's event. And you were reviewing the bad guys' faces to be sure you had never seen them. Before making that a formal statement to that."

"I told you he's a cop," Abby muttered.

"I have already seen the pictures myself, and there does not seem to be much to do in your review. From here, it is just a formality there were multiple security cameras that captured the entire shooing, with that much coverage you won't have a problem."

"Now wait a chicken-picking minute. The guy I shot had the drop on my partner, but because I shot him in the kitchen, I get delayed. Next time I shoot someone, maybe I will do it during halftime at the Super Bowl."

Ivy smiled, and his child-like oversized eyes flashed at Abby. "Relax, I am not here to bust anyone's chops. I need a small favor."

This statement drew both Abby and Lavon to the edge of their seats.

"O'Leary wants to question both of you separately with Lieutenant Nash in the room. I would like to know if I can sit in."

"Why?" Abby asked.

"I want to know if the evening events are related to something I have been working on."

"The fact that you are intelligence, and you are asking is a formality. I would love to have you join me in my session." Lavon answered.

For a moment, Abby seemed distracted by something she was reading as she casually opened her incoming mail. She read it, then reread it as if the white spaces between the lines held cues to what the letter was about. Abby looked up and noticed both men had stopped talking and were now waiting for her answer.

"Yeah, sure, Lvy, I got issues with many people but not with you. The more, the merrier."

ABBY ONLY HAD A MOMENT to wonder about the questions O'Leary might be asking her partner. The note she had received distracted her. It was a note from the court clerk stating that she was being removed from any case that was assigned to Judge Lynn Dodd-Masterson. This was a problem, she thought, but could she ask Lavon why his girlfriend pulled her? Was it Abby's flippant remarks that now irritated Lynn?

The new arrangement of the seating played its second trick of the morning; as Abby looked up, there was a young man in his early to mid-twenties staring at her. He was handsome and seemed almost familiar. He was holding two white boxes. The young man wore jeans and a plaid shirt.

"Don't feel bad, kid. It's a new building. I still get lost. You want to go down that hall and make a right. There is a sign that says Men's. You can go in there and shake the snake." Abby looked back at the note from the courts.

"I'm not lost, Abby. I am sorry if I was staring. Momma didn't tell me how powerfully attractive you are. I guess it took me by surprise." He sat the boxes on Abby's desk.

"Is this the part where I call the bomb squad?"

"And generous too to be willing to share with those boys."

"No, wait a minute. Good looking. A dreadful county accent. You know my name. And you speak about Momma." A surprised look overtook Abby's face. "That can only mean one thing. You are one of the 500 brothers of Porter Wagner." Abby sprang to her feet. Abby then threw herself into the young man's arms and gave him a big hug. Finally, something about this day was looking up.

"Ma'am, I really enjoy this embrace, but since I don't know that Porter fella, I won't want to be stealing something that belongs to another man."

"Cute as the dickens and dumb as a box of rocks. No doubt you are Lavon's brother."

"Yes, Ma'am. My name is Lovester."

"Lester, do you know that means there is a real cake in that box." Abby released Lovester and started searching her drawer for silverware.

"Lovester." He attempted to correct it.

"Yeah, that's what I said." She said with a mouth full of cake. "Real cake. I ate a bit out of a fake cake last night, and I have to get the shitty taste out of my mouth." Abby waved and continued to devour the cake.

"You should sit or something; your brother is in the principal's office getting a spanking. He should be pulling his pants up any moment."

"Humor is different here in the big city, I see."

"What kind of pigeonhole could you come from that makes Shepherd Pass seem like the big city?" Abby began examining the other box, and it contained a pecan pie. Abby rolled her eyes with delight.

"Momma says you have been feeling ill at spirits, and you deserve a reward for dealing with a Tyler male on a day-by-day basis with none of the side benefits. Whatever that means."

"Hey, partner, looks who's here. It's your brother, Lester," Abby called out as she saw Lavon and Ivy approaching.

"Lovester." Lavon half corrected and half greeted his brother. "Why are you here?"

"Miss Blackwell, I think we have the next dance," Ivy stated in an apparent attempt to leave the two brothers alone. Lvy begins leading Abby to the meeting with Don Nash and Detective O'Leary.

"I came to tell you face to face that I forgive you for the inappropriate romantic goings on with you and my fiancée at the time." Abby could hear Lovester starting the conversation.

"Alight, hold the heck on. This is better than any meeting," Abby turned back to the brothers to hear Lavon's response.

"I never laid a hand on Shavon." Lavon protested.

"Shavon. Shavon, why does that name sound familiar?" Abby searched her brain.

"Abby, let's let these boys have some privacy," Ivy suggested.

"Shavon. That's Calamity Jane." Abby realized who Lovester's fiancée was. "Wait a minute, he is upset because he thinks you hung ten in the nut case."

"Abby, we have other work, and you aren't helping," Ivy suggested to Abby.

"Oh, I understand the two of them alone here in the big city. Working some dangerous cases together. Some evenings, it just happens." Lovester romanticized.

"Slow down, Sonny Jim Jr. What happened was your girl was working for an angry gangster on the turf of another gangster without his permission, I might add. She and her boss withheld evidence that causes all manner of mayhem." Abby began changing the version of events. "Now, we could ask her boss, but they are still scraping what's left of her off the side of Patrick's Bar and Grill with a mop and a scrub pad."

"Abby, please go to the meeting; we can talk later," Lavon instructed Abby.

"Guard my cake," Abby commanded, walking off with Ivy.

Abby and Ivy walked toward Nash's office, and Abby suddenly stopped and turned to Ivy with questions on her face.

"What is it, Abby?"

"Can I ask you a question?"

"Sure."

"I got a notice from the courts that Judge Masterson is recusing me. She won't take any case I have. That means since all the other judges have their caseloads, my cases go to the back of the pile. A bunch of shitheads I spent my good time arresting will get to walk around a little longer."

"Where is the question?"

"If Lavon's girlfriend is feeling jealous of our relationship, maybe it's time for him to get a male partner. What do you think."

A couple of Detectives in a two-person cubical were discussing something on a map with a uniformed officer, and they did not notice the conversation between Ivy and Abby; Ivy still huddled closer to Abby to assure privacy.

"Well, so I can answer, do me a favor first and answer this question. In the meeting with Lavon, he told us you saved his life."

Abby looked down at the floor as if ashamed of herself.

"So, say Lavon Tyler had a different partner—a man not quite as instinctually wound as you. How do you feel waking up every morning with one side of the bed ice cold, where she refused to sleep as if she thought he might be coming home? Judge Masterson would feel. But of course, he never would."

Horror quickly overtook Abby's face, and the signs of selfishness evaporated completely.

"Need a moment to think about that one. Fair enough. Different question. How would you feel staring down at Lavon in a casket, thinking you could have saved him if you had been there."

"Damn you, Ivy. You really know how to be a prick."

"How do you think I got this job? I hear he saved your life a little while back in a hotel lobby."

Abby's eyes met Lvy's. He could see Abby beyond the jocularity. A real person. Just not one willing to expose her inner being to any and everyone.

Through the glass doors of Nash's office, Nash and O Leary could see Abby Ivy had stopped to confer. They began motioning for them to enter the room.

"Do me a favor, Ivy, don't tell him I even thought about switching partners.

And don't let anyone know we talk to each other like real people occasionally."

"It will be our secret, but you have to promise me you won't let people know I am not always a jerk."

ABBY'S MEETING TOOK twice as long as Lavon's, and they were sure nothing good came from their meetings.

"Where is my cake and pie?" Abby growled at Lavon upon her return.

"I put it away. I don't want you to ruin your lunch."

"That is my lunch."

"No. We have been invited to have lunch with Dolan Dodd."

"I don't have my primary weapon back, and neither do you. And are not supposed to be actively working this case."

"Maybe we should try not to kill anyone and just have lunch. Besides, I told Nash that if I spoke to Dolan, I would ask him to speak with the cops doing the investigation. Think of it as a goodwill mission."

"THERE ARE MY HEROES." JoAnn Dodd yelled out as Lavon and Abby walked across the lawn to the mansion. The lunch had been arranged at Dolan's estate rather than his office building. JoAnn put one arm around Lavon's waist and then looped the other through Abby's arm. JoAnn had recently been in a state of mourning following the death of her lover.

Today, the mourning veil had been lifted or at least given a reprieve.

Lavon was somewhat confused about why JoAnn seemed to take to him unreservedly.

She had once told him she reminded him of Dolan when he was younger. There was a grand courtyard with a fountain with a sculpture of a dragon shooting water from its mouth. An elegant outdoor table had been set, with plenty of wait staff. Upon arrival, Abby and Lavon noticed many guards patrolling the grounds. When Lavon and Abby reached the dining table, a man about their age in a herringbone three-piece suit walked out. The man was slightly taller than Lavon and equally muscular. He had brown hair and hazel eyes that seemed to flash. He reached over to shake Lavon's hand.

"I am Nicolas Braden; my friends call me Nicky. I work for a law firm doing business with Mr. Dodd. I hope you don't mind my joining your lunch."

"Not at all. We aren't investigating. We just came to the free food."

Abby answered and then jumped, startled by a young woman who seemed to appear from nowhere dressed precisely like Nicky.

Abby did a double take.

"It's called twins. I am sure you have them here. I am Nicole, and you can call me Cole."

Abby was about to make a flippant remark when the twins removed their jackets in what looked like choreographed consistency. They were both wearing shoulder holsters with Glocks in them.

"You know most of the lawyers I know don't wear firearms." Lavon comment.

"That is because the Braden twins are not lawyers. They are investigators for a full-service law firm."

The baritone explanation came from the door as Dolan Dodd, the robust and broad man who looked like an enforcer in his mid-life, walked from the doorway. On his arm was a small, framed woman with blond hair. The young woman wore a tight shirt that revealed her figure and tattoos. Dolan's young escort immediately began eyeing Abby.

"Your hair is amazing." The young woman started toward Abby, and Cole stepped between the two.

"This is Libby. She is our friend and associate and promised to behave herself."

Libby projected a look like a scolded child but desisted her pursuit for the time. Lavon and Abby exchange a, what the hell did we sign up for look?

Lunch was excellent. There was steak and lobster. Nicky and Lavon both had a knowledge of boxing that kept them talking. Cole said little, as did Libby, but Libby seemed genuinely interested in observing Abby's every movement.

"I brought you presents," Libby announced at the end of the meal. "Case each of the Pettibone Brandy."

"We can't accept gifts for doing our jobs. And my partner can't drink."

Lavon replied.

"That is not quite true. You can accept a gift if no favor is attached and there is no expectation of future reciprocity." Nicky corrected. "Libby is giving you a gift, and you don't know her, and she has no expectation of you doing her a favor in the future."

"And I can drink. I choose not to." Abby corrected that part of Lavon's statement as well.

Lavon was sure he had misspoken by the expression on Abby's face, but that would have to wait.

"I had your brandy delivered to the mansion where you stay." Libby leaned forward as if Lavon was far away. Then she turned and leaned in toward Abby. "I will just have to find something you like, and maybe we can get together privately and pick something out." Libby batted her eyes at Abby.

The moment had come, and Lavon was sure of it—explaining why the lunch had been called.

"Tell me, Detective Tyler, if you were the policeman investigating the attempted murder last night, what would stick out at you the most?" Nicky asked.

"I am not, and I only came to ask Mr. Dodd to cooperate with the police that are investigating."

"It is hypothetical; please answer my brother. We have a bet." Cole requested.

Everyone around the table started staring at Lavon like his following words would be mystical.

"Okay. Have you ever been to a square dance?"

The crowd relaxed at the questions, all but Nicky.

"Never."

"Well, it looks like mass confusion to an outside observer. Then the fiddler calls allemande left or dosado, and everyone makes the same move simultaneously." Lavon smiled at his explanation.

"What the hell does that mean?" Abby was more confused that Nicky and Cole understood the explanation, and apparently, Dolan and JoAnn did as well.

"Sweetheart, your partner is saying in a room full of waiters, bus boys, athletes, and staff from over fifteen feet away, someone lined Mr. Dodd up for a clear shot," Cole explained.

"Oh, shit, someone called Allemande left or Dosado, and the bodyguard stepped to the left, allowing the shooter a clear lane of fire." Like a bolt from the blue, the reality hit Abby.

"It is the same open lane your partner used to whack that scum-sucking dog." Dolans uttered in his deep voice.

Cole reached into her purse, pulled out a ten-dollar bill, and handed it to her brother. Nicky reached into the inside pocket of his jacket, pulled out a slip of paper, and gave it to Lavon.

"What is this?"

"Why, it's the names and addresses of the bodyguards covering Mr. Dodd."

"You see, Nicky boy, your special talent won't be needed. I have seen Detective Tyler in action. He will eradicate any threat." JoAnn smiled.

After lunch, as Lavon and Abby prepared to leave, Dolan pulled Lavon to the side. "I want to give you a gift, too."

"It isn't necessary."

"The gift comes in the form of some good advice." Dolan continued as Lavon's protest had fallen like a snowflake on a hot grill. "Someone is going to offer you something too good to be true. It's a setup." And with that, Dolan was gone.

On the drive back, Abby kept staring out the window and not speaking.

"I'm sorry, Abby."

"About what?"

"About whatever I said or did back there that upset you."

"Typical of men. You know you did something stupid, but you are not only too stupid to admit you don't know what you said or did. But you are too stupid to wait and see if it is important."

"Well, you could tell me. That way, I won't do it again."

Abby waited as if considering whether to let Lavon off the hook. "Look, you said I can't drink. I can drink. I choose not to. Every day, an alcoholic makes a choice not to drink. Some days are harder than others, but we must choose for ourselves. The choice can't be conditional or for someone else. It must be because we chose it."

Abby seemed satisfied that Lavon understood how he had misspoken, and the mod in the vehicle got lighter. "What were you and Dodd whispering about?"

"He was giving me some sort of warning. I have a feeling I will know exactly what he was talking about when the time arises." Lavon smiled. "Think the little girl has a crush on you."

"I don't do girls, Homer."

"You know we could go left and back to the station or right and introduce ourselves to one of these square-dancing bodyguards."

"Well, it's right then; got to dance off some of that lobster."

LAVON CREPT SLOWLY down the passenger's side of the new Mercedes parked in the driveway of the home where the address for the bodyguard was listed. He had his backup weapon in his hand pointed toward the ground. Abby approached simultaneously from the driver's side of the vehicle. Abby had her backup weapon, an old Smith and Wesson six short snub nose revolver pointed at the driver's side of the car. There was someone in the front seat of the vehicle.

Before arriving, Lavon and Abby had used the car radio to check firearm permits and the general information for Reinhart Sheldon, the first of the two bodyguards assigned to protect Dolan Dodd on the night of the incident. Sheldon was listed on his last driver's license renewal as 340 pounds and six foot four feet tall. Since Dolan Dodd was a broad man, it took a wide, massive man to cover him. Sheldon had several guns listed, but his car had to be brand new.

"I told you we should have called for backup. This guy is a monster." Abby whispered to Lavon.

"That would mean we were working the case. We are not."

"Is that your dick in your hand?"

Before Lavon could formulate an answer, he had reached a point where he could see the car's front window. He could see a hole in the car's front window. Lavon looked in from the passenger side of the vehicle and could see a corresponding hole in the forehead of the passenger.

"Please leave my dick out of our conversations." Lavon requested as he could see Abby catching a glimpse of their latest problem.

"Speaking of your dick, what did you do with your brother?"

Lavon leaned forward to catch a better look at a grocery bag on the seat beside the deceased Rinehart Sheldon.

"I told Lynn he is in town, and she wants him to stay at the mansion rather than one of the low-end hotels." Lavon's focus was split between answering Abby and the bag on the seat. It was moving. Lavon moved his face closer to the car window, and a small head popped out and stared back at him. It was a tiny white kitten that had gotten hungry and was pillaging the bag for any food it could find a way to open.

"Call the station and tell them to be quick, or I am going to break out the windows. And have them get O'Leary out here." Lavon commanded with agitation in his voice.

Chapter 3

"**W**hy are the two trying to screw up my investigation?" Detective O'Leary screamed as he joined the large group of police and technicians Examining the crime scene. Nash was with a group trying to figure out the trajectory of the sniper fire that had killed Sheldon.

"Don't yell at us because you run a crappy investigation. When someone asked my partner who he should be questioning, he started with the bodyguards. Where did you start the girls' volleyball team."

"There are over three hundred people that must be questioned. Maybe if I were screwing one of the Dodds, I would have inside information on ...."

Before O'Leary could finish his statement, Lavon lunged forward to grab him. Abby was between the two men and had to charge Lavon to stop him from tackling O'Leary. A couple of uniformed officers saw Abby trying to restrain Lavon. They were required to stop Lavon from reaching O'Leary.

"Stand down, Detective." Don Nash appeared.

"Hey Nash, tell this guy saying nasty things about a significant other is out of line." Abby was rumpled from wrestling with Lavon, and her dark, curly hair covered her face.

Nash looked at the two angry men. "You got time to play name-calling games. It looks to me like your best lead has a hole in his head." Then Nash looked at Lavon and Abby. "FBI Agent Patterson is requesting your presents ASAP. He says he will meet you at your desk. And by the way, a really shitty job of not being involved in this case."

WHEN LAVON AND ABBY reached their cubical, Patterson was sitting in Abby's seat, reading the note from the court clerk.

"It is illegal to read other people's mail, not to mention rude as hell." Abby snapped.

"No harm intended." Agent Patterson passed a look from Abby to Lavon, then dismissed it as he stood. "So, I know where to start. Are you two seeking a career in FBI Major Case, or are you planning to be world-class hitmen?"

Lavon and Abby stared at each other as if the other had the missing piece of the puzzle that would make more sense out of the dialog.

"Let me ask this way: Are you working for Ivy?"

Lavon settled into his seat and waited for Abby to do the same. "Sorry, I am just as lost as when this conversation started, if you can call it a conversation."

Moments of silence passed.

"Well, at least tell me how the lobster was?"

"You are reading my mail, and you are following us." Abby raged.

"No, if I were following you, I would know why the two of you look like you have been wrestling. No detective, I have people at the airport who tell me when a certain tail number lands in or near Shepherds Pass."

"They have their own plane. I got to be in the wrong business?" Abby started, and Lavon laughed. Lavon was beginning to forget the altercation of the evening.

"The firm they work with has five planes that move across the country."

"Have you ever encountered a wolf in the wild that does not run with a pack?" Lavon asked.

"Can't say as I have," Patterson answered.

"There is a look in his eyes that tells you he is a killer and does not need any help or provocation outside rules as he sees them."

"You saw that look in the eyes of the twins," Abby revealed. "What did you see in the eyes of the little blond?" Abby asked.

"Wait, you mean to tell me they had Libby Pettibone with them?" Patterson sang out excitedly.

"Pettibone, why does that name sound familiar?" Lavon searched his recollection.

"Pettibone Wineries and Pettibone Distilleries. The kid has control of the whole fortune. She also runs messages between some gangsters that are not allowed back into this country."

Lavon smiled at Abby.

"Oh no, don't you dare sit there with that smug look on your face, redneck?"

"What am I missing.?" Patterson asked.

"She has a crush on Abby."

Patterson looked at Abby and shook his head as if he was trying to shake something loose. "Be careful with her. She has quite a mysterious origin and to give you an example of what you are dealing with. Let me tell you a little story. Nicky breaks Vivian's heart. Vivian gets pissed and has a large guy beat up Cole's boyfriend. Rumor is Libby handled it."

"How did it turn out?" Abby asked.

"I'll answer that when we find Vivian's head."

"What?" Lavon and Abby said in unison.

"What part of that did you not get?"

"You are saying that spacey little chick decapitates people. Excuse me if I am wrong but shouldn't you guys' arrest people for shit like that." Abby shrieked.

"That is where lines get a little murky. See, the first thing you must learn if you two are going to work my side of the street is there are lakes of things people know to happen. But when you are looking for evidence to take to court, you cannot find enough to fill a thimble. For example, your friend the wolf killed 31 people in one evening to rescue a district attorney and his wife and daughter. Still, no one wanted to say a word about it because our guys were pursuing the wrong guys and prosecuting him would make them look like the Keystone cops."

"They didn't kill Sheridan," Lavon announced.

"How do you know?" Patterson asked.

"Today at lunch, JoAnn told them their skills would not be needed. And he handed me the list. He thought Sheridan was still alive."

"Good because they went wheels up an hour after your fancy meal." Patterson stood to leave. "One other thing, Amber Dodd is requesting your presence."

"Why." The question came from Abby like she was racing Lavon to it.

"Maybe you can tell me after you speak to her. My boss says make it happen."

ABBY STEPPED OUT OF her old Nissan and noticed a tear in her jacket. The minor rip had come to no doubt from her wrestling with Lavon. Abby stood looking down at the tare, now remembering only the energy she shared while wrestling with Lavon as passion flowed through him, even if the current in no way led to her. "Get it out of your head, girl." She muttered to herself."

Abby lived in a two-story apartment building in the lower eighteen blocks of Shepherds Pass. Abby lived only with Cletus, her English Bulldog puppy. Something out of place caught her eye as she walked toward the building. A slight flicker of her curtain. The type of thing most people dismiss. There should be no one in her apartment. Her instincts would not let her ignore the anomaly.

"Cletus has been practicing a trick all day, and I think he wants to show you." Babette, one of Abby's first-floor neighbors, met her as she entered the building. Babette was about twelve years old and in her homely phase, with acne and thick glasses. Babette carried Cletus like a baby, and Cletus propelled himself from Babette to land in Abby's arms the moment he saw her.

"Babette, I need you to take Cletus for a little while longer, and I need to borrow your mother's mop."

Abby walked casually up the stairs leading to the second floor. She took off her jacket and unscrewed the light bulb in the hallway. Now, only a dim light from the moon showed through a window at the reverse end of the hall. Abby stopped at her door, took out her keys, and giggled them. She removed her backup Smith and Wesson from her purse and laid it on the floor outside the apartment door. She then took the jack and put it over the borrowed mop. Abby kneeled to the left of the door, turned the key in the lock, and pushed the door open, exposing the jacket on the end of the mop.

Boom. A thunderous explosion sounded. The fake Abby was shattered in two. Boom. A second shot rang. It was a pump shotgun; Abby could tell by the cocking sound between the shots. The shotgun fired, and the burst's reflection made a flash with sparks that lit the room. Abby dived into the room and fired two shots into the massive flash she had seen. A huge mass fell backward, and she heard the shotgun drop. But in the darkness, Abby could see the heavy mass that had fired the shotgun had fallen back into another mass. Shit, there are at least two of them, she thought. Abby raised her gun hand as high as she could and fired twice at where she thought the second assassin should be. Then she ducked, hoping that he could not see her if she could not see him. He would have to rely on the mussel flashes like she did. Abby ducked and rolled just in time to miss a volley of automatic gunfire. Abby rose to her knees and fired the remaining two shots from the Smith and Wesson revolver.

"Damn." A man's voice cried out in pain.

Abby knew two critical things. One was that she had hit him. And two, her gun was empty. Abby did a rapid commando crawl for the shotgun she had heard hit the ground. Abby recovered the shotgun and cranked a round into the chamber. The percussion of the shotgun vaulted Abby back and landed her on the body of the first mass. The explosion seemed timed with the breaking of glass and the splintering of wood. The second shooter had jumped from her second-story window. Abby sprang to her feet and tried to race to the window but slid into a pool of blood and fell to one knee. She scrambled to the window in time to see a man half running and half limping running down the alley.

"Stop all that racket. I am going to call the police." Abby could hear one of her elderly neighbors screaming through the walls.

"I am the cops. Dial 911. I need help." Abby stood in the dark, picking glass shards from her minor wounds.

Chapter 4

"Detective Blackwell, would it do any good to ask how you are doing?" Wendell asked. Wendell arrived as the sergeant on the scene and ordered patrol cars to canvas the area.

"I am fine, sergeant."

"Your partner is on his way up. He was sniffing blood splatter in the alley."

"What?"

"Some manhunter thing."

LAVON ENTERED THE APARTMENT and spread a map on Abby's table. "Your guys are patrolling this area." He verified with Wendell.

"Yep, no way he makes it to the lower nine blocks."

"I want you to get on the radio and see if there is any activity here." Lavon circled an area on the map.

LAVON WALKED TO ABBY, who stood in an old bathrobe clutching Cletus. "Your hair is a mess." Lavon reached forward and brushed blood-stained hair from her face.

"Got it," Wendell yelled, reentering the room. "Carjacking right where you pointed on the map. The victims say the guy was bleeding and in pain. Also carrying some form of machine gun."

"We got to go now," Lavon announced to Wendell.

"Let me find some bullets for this, Smith," Abby stated.

"No, Abby, you must stay here for the crime scene investigation. If you leave, you get suspended, and I need you to watch my back. I got a strong feeling this mess is just starting."

"I got his back, Wendell announced."

Abby stared at Wendell, knowing he and Lavon were right. "Bring him back with as much as a paper cut, and I will hunt you down."

"YOU CAN'T GO IN THERE. There is a man with a gun in there. He says he is going to shoot everybody." An old woman with a walker stumbled to pass Lavon and Wendell as they strolled across the Shepherd Pass General Hospital parking lot toward the emergency entrance. People fled as fast as they could, headed in the opposite direction of Lavon and Wendell.

"I certainly hope so, ma'am, or we came to the wrong place," Lavon answered.

"You guys need backup?" An old security guard in a crumpled blue uniform asked as he noticed Wendell's police uniform.

"Nah. We got this." Lavon answered, following the direction the guard pointed out.

A dozen or so people were crouching and trying to stay out of the line of fire when Lavon and Wendell entered the room. The gunman had one arm around the neck of a young candy striper. The gunman was bleeding and in apparent pain, with his back to a counter holding himself up. The gunman was a big man with an angry look and a stern face with eyes that surveyed the room constantly.

"One more move, cop, and I start spraying the room."

"You will do no such thing," Lavon stated, then looked at the distressed people. "Is everybody alright?" People began shaking their heads, signaling a negative response. "Your day seems to be going as bad as mine." Lavon addressed the gunman.

The gunman looked at Wendell, who was pointing his gun at him. "Where did you guys have to go to find a real cowboy."

"I find that highly insulting. I am not a cowboy. I am from Mississippi. Not Texas, Arizona, or Wyoming. Why is it that whenever people hear a little accent, they start thinking about cowboys?"

"Is he always like this?" The gunman asked Wendell.

"Pretty much. We had to stop him from beating up another one of the cops earlier. The last time he did that he beat the guys so bad; he will never be physically able to return to duty."

"Great. I took this job on short notice and ended up in a town full of nut jobs." The man complained in a Brooklyn accent.

Lavon looked around the room. "What can I call you, sir?"

"Walter."

"Well, Walter, let me be perfectly honest with you. My main reason for being here tonight is to keep you alive."

This revelation drew stares from Wendell and Walter.

"Explain." Walter insisted.

"Well, if you see that clock on the wall. If you promise not to shoot anybody or anything for five minutes, I will be happy to explain my position."

"Kid, you got it, this I got to hear."

Lavon put his gun in his waistband.

"You can't do that, Lavon," Wendell complained.

"Well, we have his word. Now, if I wanted you dead, being a fairly good shot and considering you are a foot taller than that little girl, I could have shot you in the head long ago." Lavon searched the faces of the hostages, watching and listening, like they were a jury weighing his argument.

"I guess." Walter had to agree.

"See, in a little more than five minutes, the swat team will be here. Their motto is We kill shit. They will drive through wall in a mini tank. Come swing in on ropes. And start lobbing flash bangs and tear gas grenades."

"Holly shit."

"Your second option is to shoot us and head for the street. But that is just as bad because there are about a hundred cops out there who are looking for their first righteous kill. And you could be that. First righteous kill is like an exclusive club for cops."

"This is getting scary. But I think I see you aren't afraid."

'The other issue is that you said you got this job as a late fill-in. Your assignment failed. Do you really think the people above you are going to step up and admit it was their fault? Even if you get out of here, they must whack you as a loose end so that no one knows they screwed up."

"I hate to say it, but you are making sense, kid."

"I got to pee." The little candy striper squealed, wiggling to hold it in.

"Wendell, take her to go pee," Lavon instructed.

"Wait, I haven't made up my mind. What choice are you offering." Walter asked.

"Well, you only got a minute or so left. Do you want her peeing on you while you think?"

"Wendell, take her and get the rest of these people out of here, too," Walter instructed.

"I can't leave you." Wendell insisted.

"That's an order, sergeant," Lavon commanded Wendell and began hustling the hostages out to the room. "And Wendell, tell them to have swat stand down."

"What's next?" Walter asked when he and Lavon were alone. Walter's energy had started to waiver, and his injuries were becoming more of an issue.

"Now, you let me arrest you. That way you will be technically in my custody, I have to try and keep you alive."

"Can you tell me why keeping me alive is so important to you?"

"One of the other detectives is working on a case that I think has something to do with the job you had tonight and keeping you alive will piss him off."

"That sounds evil."

"Besides, right now, I like you much more than I like him."

"I guess you got to cuff me."

"Maybe later, why don't you put your arm around my shoulders, and I find you an examination room."

"HOW ARE YOU FEELING now, Walter?" Joan Patterson asked Walter. He did not answer immediately; it took a moment for him to get his bearings. He was aware he had drifted off while being helped by Lavon. Dr. Patterson is married to FBI Agent Patterson and is a Lavon and Lynn's friend.

"When we heard Lavon had guests in the house, we rushed right down." Nya, a nurse married to Wendell, spoke from opposite the bed. "You are a fortunate man."

"So why don't I feel like I won the lottery?"

"Nya means because few people get in a gunfight with Abby and live to talk about it." Joan filled in.

"So, if everybody knows this bitch is really Wyatt Earp in drag, how did someone forget to tell me." Walter noticed Lavon standing in the corner. "So, is this where you question me and get your pound of flesh?"

"No questions. I am going home, and hope Lynn is not mad at me for not calling. I have two officers assigned to watch you, but it is more for your protection than anything else. Some detectives may come to ask you questions. You don't have to answer anything without a lawyer.

And I instructed the guys I have watching over you to stay in the room if the Detective comes and tapes the conversations."

Chapter 5

"Thank you for letting me sleep on the way up here." Lavon had done the drive, and Abby had fallen asleep when the truck pulled out of the police station garage. They were standing in the Chillicothe Correctional Center, and Lavon had just come from his third search. He was tempted to tell the woman who insisted on searching him a third time that he had not sprouted or grown anything different from the first two searches.

But he knew women endured far greater humiliations and trained themselves to push to them to back of their minds every day.

"No problem, you probably didn't get any sleep."

"No, I think every cop in town stopped by last night. With every tech and medical examiner. Hell, even Ivy stopped by."

A guard began leading them down a hallway to the secured interview rooms.

"What is Ivy's story?" Lavon asked.

"Sorry. Like I told you before, he is too smart for me to figure out. Reminds me a lot of you in a way."

Lavon noticed the interview room was nothing special. It looked quite like the interview rooms in the new police station. There was a metal table in the center with rods for securing prisoners while being questioned.

The walls were padded, and there were small windows for observers who chose not to be in the room. Amber Dodd and Lynn Dodd

Masterson were cousins. Lavon had lived with Lynn for months, so he had seen her without her makeup many times. It startled him how much Amber looked like an unmade-up version of Lynn. Two guards led Amber into the room and shackled and chained her to the table.

Amber stared directly at Lavon after she was seated.

"The FBI says you want to speak with us." Lavon began.

"No, I want to speak to you. She is along for the ride." Amber made no effort to look at Abby.

"You, making a lot of new girlfriends here, Amber?" Abby asked.

"You see, Detective Tyler, I sat up last night thinking of all the smart-mouth things a drunken last pick of a whore could say to rattle me. I thought of what my responses should be."

"And what did you come up with?" Abby asked.

"Just this. I did everything I did in Shepherds Pass right under your nose for years. You never had a clue. If it weren't for your partner, I would still be piling up bodies and skimming millions from both sides of the family. The one thing I could not have planned years ago when this all started was that a broken-hearted country boy would show up to save the day. So do us the courtesy of shutting the fuck up while we decide how to proceed from here."

"You say proceed like this is an open negotiation. You are smart enough to know I don't have the power to offer you anything. And without your lawyer in the room, I wouldn't try even if I did."

Amber stared at Lavon as if there was a secret meaning he would suddenly uncover. "I heard you saved Dolan Dodds's life."

"We were just doing our jobs."

"Let me tell you what would have happened if you had not stopped that assignation." Amber smiled. "Constantine Dodd, his son, would have been forced to come home and run things."

"I take it that is a bad thing."

Amber's eyes shifted to Abby. "Constantine Dodd is a much larger problem than his father." Abby introjected.

"How?"

"Well, my dear Detective Tyler, since you are new in these parts, let me outline it for you. Constantine doesn't respect the rule of order for organized crime families. He hates politicians, and he has great and powerful enemies."

"Sounds like King Kong. But what does that have to do with me?"

"Don't you see, when you stopped me from neutralizing both sides of the family, you added to the balance of power? I wanted to explain that you must do whatever you can, legal or illegal, to preserve the balance between both sides of the family."

Lavon could feel himself being swirled into a logic tidal pool. There was information he needed to grasp to keep from being sucked under by the deadly undercurrent, but he had no idea what he should be asking. "What are you asking for, Amber?"

"My life. Nothing more."

This request caused both Lavon and Abby to settle back into the uncomfortable chairs of the interview room.

"I had time to think about it since I have been in here. You fell in love. You genuinely think you saved the day. You solved a bunch of murderers. But baby, you are part of the reason a storm is headed this way."

"LUCY," ABBY EXCLAIMED as she viewed a large black woman behind the registration desk. Abby raced to the woman. "So, this is where they have been keeping you."

Lucy was a large woman with facial features that more resembled those common to a man's face than a woman. She had a broad nose, angry eyes, and a mouth that seemed plastered on her face. "Yeah, I drew an 18-month suspension pending review."

"Tyler, Lucy is a Shepherds Pass Street cop, or at least she was."

Lavon was surprised Abby introduced him under his real name but did not mention it.

"You look a lot better than the last time I saw you."

"New moisturizer." Abby lied.

"Is this good-looking thing your new squeeze?" Lucy gave Lavon's a once over.

"No. He is my partner. He has a girlfriend."

"He looks like a guy that can handle two."

"I think so too, but so far, no squeezing. What do you know about Amber Dodd and her stay at your five-star hotel here?"

Lucy's large eyes panned the room as if she was about to pass on nuclear launch codes. "She has access to money. She pays for protection, so no one messes with her here."

"Is she paying inmates or guards?" Lavon whispered.

"Are you wearing a wire?"

"If I was, I am sure one of the many women that felt me up would have found it by now." Lavon complained.

"Comes with being so damn cute, fella." Lucy winked. "Both."

"Any visitors other than the lawyer?" Abby asked.

"That information requires a written request. But I need to refill my water jug. If I turn to the page and leave the book here for a minute, you might see what you are looking for."

"Do you mind if I ask why, you got suspended?" Lavon asked as Lucy looked up the page in a large logbook.

"My supervisor on the job was telling a joke. What is the difference between a colored girl and a sorry as nigger bitch?"

"How did the joke end?"

"It ended with me knocking his puck ass out. No regrets. I will be back in a minute."

"I like her," Lavon commented to Abby. The moment of glee was short as they checked out the name on the logbook. There was only one other than the law firm personnel.

Paden Dodd.

Chapter 6

Lavon and Abby entered Paden's Place, the smokehouse restaurant owned by Paden Dodd. Abby had been reluctant to enter the restaurant because of past ill will between her and Paden; Abby, however, was unwilling to let Lavon out of her site while investigating whatever they were now immersed in.

"You can stay, but you have to leave your Bitch outside. I don't allow dogs in here. We serve food." Paden met Lavon as he entered the restaurant. She wore a cooking apron. She was followed closely by a large Native American Indian. The restaurant was filled with guests. The customers seemed to be from all ages, and no racial group was left unrepresented. The young teens played a video game in the corner of the place, and an atmosphere of covariance was pervasive throughout the smokehouse.

Lavon and Abby missed at least one meal in the transition involving their travel to collect information. Their stomachs grumbled in unison as the smell of fresh smoke, brisket, and chicken wings permeated the air.

"She is a police detective, and my partner she stays," Lavon stated.

"No, don't worry. I will watch you from the patio." Abby started heading out toward the patio. Abby's meek acquiescence surprised Lavon, but he did not want to lose control of the opportunity to question Paden.

Shortly after Lavon was seated at the table, Paden reappeared with a heaping plate of food for Lavon and sat it in front of him. Paden motioned, and one of the servers brought sweet tea and sat a pitcher and two glasses at the table.

"I am starved, and this food looks to die for, but I can't eat knowing my partner is starving." Lavon proclaimed.

"I will have a plate sent out to her, Uncle Lavon." Paden offered and gestured to the server.

"I think you are supposed to call me Detective Tyler."

"Are you sleeping with Lynn?"

"This is not your business or why I came, but the obvious answer is yes."

"Are you living in the same house?"

"Second, yes. But..."

"But unless you are going to say she is just a cheap piece of ass until you can find something better. I suggest you accept my offer to consider you family." Paden's comment and much of the venom her grandfather had displayed when he first misunderstood the loving relationship between Lavon and Lynn.

"Since we find ourselves unable to avoid this topic completely, let me tell you the same thing I told your grandfather." Lavon paused and waited for some of the mounting consternation to discharge from her face. "I have never slept with a woman that I have not have romantic feelings toward. And I would like to add that our feelings toward each other are best worked through between her and me without the assistance of others."

Paden reached across the table and took Lavon's hand. "Good because she loves you, and she deserves to be happy. Now you can ask your questions."

"Your name was the name that came up as having visited Amber Dodd. What did you discuss if it is not too personal?"

"She asked for me to visit her. She sent a request through her lawyer."

"Did she say why?"

"No, and to be honest, I thought maybe she wanted to deal. Give back more of the money she stole. In exchange for..." Paden looked down, not sure whether to finish the statement.

"For her life," Lavon confirmed he knew the missing part of the statement.

Lavon had been eating and watching Abby on the patio. A slender Blackman walked to Abby, and it took a moment for Lavon to remember where he knew the man. He was Detron Clark one of the local paramedics. Detron was a tall thin black man with long braids. Detron entered with a woman who seemed to be confronting Abby about something but since there were beyond the glass, Lavon could not hear the conversation. Just as Lavon was about to stand and walkout side to be sure Abby was alright, Abby stooked and poured a full glass on the crotch of the paramedic. The woman with the paramedic seemed livid, but the paramedic led her away. Paden had stopped her information, waiting for Lavon's attention to return. "Now you see why I don't let dogs in my place."

"Are you and Amber close?"

"To tell the truth, I always wanted to be, but I always had the fear that she uses people. And I think I owe you an apology. She has, in the past, ask me questions about you. I feel guilty that maybe she is collecting information to use against you. That is why I left the meeting at the prison. She has an agenda, and I don't know what it is."

Lavon could feel Paden bonding with him, much like JoAnn Dodd. Such gentle feelings in such a rough world, the thought.

"What is the issue between you and Abby."

"Old dirt. If she wants to clean it up, I am here."

"I GUESS YOU DON'T LIKE sweet tea?" Lavon asked as he and Abby drove back to the police station. Paden had given Lavon a carryout plate to take to Lynn.

"All men are dicks." Abby proclaimed.

"I thought that was what you liked most about us." Lavon joked.

"The guy I poured the tea on, and I had been screwing from time to time."

"You don't have to confide in me, Abby."

She continued as if he had not request for her to stop. "Not like we were dating, just screwing. He is good. Real good."

"I get the picture."

"No, you don't. You see, without alcohol, I feel things."

"And you poured a drink on him because you felt jealous of the girl he was with."

"No, I poured it on him because he said don't worry, he will still have plenty left for me after he drops her off."

"What is the problem between you and Paden?"

"Past fuck up."

"What did she do?"

"Look Gomer, I told you I did fucked up things before you came to town." Abbys voice dropped and octave. "It wasn't her that fucked up it was me."

Lavon searched for a consoling word and then came up with it. "Well, look at the bright side."

"What's that."

"Well, at least you didn't shoot the paramedic."

"Well, yeah, this is that."

Chapter 7

"There you two are." Barney proclaimed as Lavon and Abby returned to the police station.

"Barney, this new building has a cafeteria," Abby stated.

"Nice to be formally meeting you, Detective Tyler." Barney continued as if he did not hear Abby.

Barney was a heavy-set Detective with a soft midsection. Barney was devouring a sub sandwich, the type that is built for the internal fixings to fall out.

"Have we met informally?"

"No. But I was in the alley the night you arrived. My first thought was oh God, another punk kid to ride on the backs of the longtime dicks like me."

"And now you don't think that is the case?" Lavon checked.

"There is a rumor going around that you gave up the booze and the one-night stands. It looks good on you, kid." Barney stated to Abby.

"Barney, this is a police station, and people usually stop by to talk cop stuff," Abby observed while cleaning up the projectile sandwich debris.

"Yeah, here is some cop stuff. Nash asked me to work with O'Leary. The other day, you two almost came to blows, and one interesting point was blurted out."

"What point?" Abby asked.

"That O'Leary is screwing up the case. He was questioning possible witnesses in alphabetical order, the way the computer prints them out. Not in order of importance. The putz is a textbook cop, not a gut-instinct kind of guy. Now his best lead has a hole in his head."

"Not our case, Barney." Lavon reminded Barney.

"Well, here is some more cop talk you might find interesting. We go to question the second bodyguard with the info you gave to Nash, and the guy vanished into a puff of smoke."

"So, he is probably concerned that Dodd will permanently terminate his employment." Lavon assessed.

"Here is the cute part. When we are leaving the guy's apartment, who should show up but Agent Patterson of the FBI with a load of questions." Barney continued eating his sandwich while Lavon and Abby stared at each other. "Here is the best part. Right after your friend from the FBI leaves, and before we can drive away, Detective Ivy, with intelligence, shows up with a list of his own questions. They both seem interested in the two of you." Barney stood and dusted the crumbs from his wrinkled suit onto the floor. "You know, Blackwell, I have a son about your age. The kid does some insurance work. He is dull as they come, but if you are planning to walk the straight and narrow, maybe he is just the kind of person you should consider. Maybe you should stop, hang out with nothing but degenerate cops, present company excluded, and think about a life outside this business."

"WAIT A MINUTE, I KNOW who you two are." A thin woman in a poorly sized business suit and wearing oversized glass stopped Lavon and Abby as they headed for Walter's room in the hospital where he was being held in police custody.

"Who are we?" Abby asked.

"I saw both of you on the news." He leaned forward and stared at Abby. "You don't look quite as deranged as you did on TV."

"Thank you."

"The news lady said that 5 minutes with you, Detective Tyler, and the two of you walked out like old fishing buddies."

"And you are?" Lavon asked.

"Koppel. Public defenders' office." She answered.

"Is your client willing to speak to us?" Lavon asked. Lavon stopped by the gift shop and picked up flowers, candy, and magazines.

"Are you kidding? He has been waiting for you. I don't know what you are up to, but his Parole Officer in Louisiana is screaming bloody murder and wants him back there for violating his parole six ways from Sunday. Do you think he will be safe in Louisiana?"

"Lady, the mod is after this guy, and he tried to kill a cop. He wouldn't be safe if he tried to hide in a different dimension." Abby sneered, pushing past Koppel to enter the room.

WHEN LAVON ENTERED the mansion, he could hear music. He heard a woman's voice. Then he heard a man's voice and knew who it was. Lovester, his brother, played musical instruments and wrote songs.

Lovester wrote when he was sad or depressed, and a heartfelt soulfulness rang out in the country duet. But before he could reach the source, of the singing, Lavon was flabbergasted by the site of the maid attempting to move a considerable crate by dragging it. "Stop that. Me and my brother can move that. What is it?"

"It was delivered here as a gift for you by a freight company. Miss Paden and your brother pried it open and took a couple of bottles of the brandy and have been singing all evening."

"Dear, great you are here. It would help if you got dressed. We have dinner with the mayor tonight. And why are people sending you crates of booze? Are you opening a liquor store?" Lynn appeared, fastening her necklace to add touches to her outfit. Lynn wore a sleek black dress that accentuated the timeless beauty that radiated from her core.

"Uncle Lavon, you're home," Paden screamed, charging toward Lavon. Paden was wearing a cut-off tee shirt that barely covered her breasts. It was clear she had no bra underneath. She wore a pair of cut-up jean shorts that exposed the cheeks of her butt. And Paden was obviously drunk.

"Whoa, slow down, young lady." Lynn intercepted Paden before she could reach Lavon. "No hugging Uncle Lavon unless you are wearing more clothes than that."

The maid concealed a chuckle, and Lynn shoved Paden to the maid. "Find somewhere for her to sleep it off."

"So, Uncle Lavon, why didn't you tell me your brother was a great magician?"

"We just met yesterday, and did you know he is also a great musician?"

"He also does magic tricks," Paden confirmed with the maid as she was led off.

"By the way, the brandy came from some little girl who has a crush on Abby."

"What?"

"I said I need to get dressed. We have dinner with the mayor."

Chapter 8

"**Y**ou know there is an old saying. The worst part of being a slave is that you know you must pass that on to your children." Mildred Lance told her son Desi as she straightened his tie. Desi was preparing for his dinner at the home of Mayor Carlton Dodd.

"Freedom is on the horizon." Desi proclaimed.

Mildred Lance stepped back to admire her prodigy.

Mildred was a middle-aged black woman with rouged good looks and an obvious intelligence you could ascertain before even speaking with her. Desi was born out of the union of his mother and a white man, and it was noticeable in his features. Desi was thin with a shy look about him. Desi's eyes tended to wander the room as if seeing something at times others missed.

"Not just your freedom, son. No more hand-me-downs or eating-the-table scraps left by people far less intelligent than you who happen to be born with the name Dodd attached."

Desi hugged his mother as if he could, through his embrace, absorb her dream for him in the future and dissipate the pain that had caused her years of secret bitterness.

"Power is your birthright, and now we have a clear plan to claim it."

WHEN LAVON ENTERED the mayor's dining room, a flash went through his mind. Clara Dodd, the mayor's wife, was here. This was conspicuous because she had made excuses not to be available during all subsequent dinners. Lavon assumed the mayor's wife may have objections to so much talk of business at the dinner table. Clara was as tall as her husband and probably the same age.

But Clara had a weathered face with age speeding to take over her remaining looks. She was stocky in such a way that made other women in the room feel comfortable about their shape. The mayor's right-hand man and public relations manager, Sean Hardcastle, was present. Lavon knew Hardcastle from past encounters and hoped his contact with the man would be limited.

"This young man is one of Shepherds Pass's future stars, Desi Lance." The mayor introduced as Lavon took notice of the unfamiliar face of the young man. Desi was in his early twenties. Desi wore a suit that looked like he wore to fit in with the conservative group he was among.

"Desi is my son from a past marriage," Hardcastle stated.

The thought was, where is that Shepherd Pass history book people have been referencing when you need it, Lavon thought. And dinner began.

The dinner had progressed nicely, but everyone at the table knew the real challenge was in front of them: navigating the conversational obstacle course.

"I hear Paden has come home. Does that mean your mother is coming for a visit?" Clara's words and tone seemed harmless enough, but Lavon could feel a chill as a shiver ran down the spine of Lynn sitting next to him.

"I suppose she will take time out for a visit soon." Lynn's cryptic answer confuses Lavon, but it is his turn for a question, and he knew it.

"I heard you and Abby Blackwell took a day trip to visit Amber Dodd in prison," Hardcastle noted. Now, like a rifle shot, Lavon knew the answer. Hardcastle and Clara Dodd never seemed to share the same dinner table because they competed for the most sensational gossip.

Lavon could feel Lynn staring at him, but he continued to eat.

"We did. That was at the request of the FBI, and we have not had time to debrief them, so I am sure you can understand if I have no idea what they feel like is confidential just yet."

Nice save rushed over Lynn's face.

"I saw you on the news; you were helping a man they say had been holding hostages," Desi questioned as if it was his turn.

Lavon seemed to search the comment for a real question, then for a concern worth addressing. "Do you believe in God?"

Lavon's questions froze everyone at the table.

"What does that have to do with anything?"

"Everything. The fact that you did not answer in a split second tells me what I need to know. I did no more or less than I had to do to bring my suspect into custody. I don't torture, maim, or needlessly humiliate anyone if I can help it. I am a servant hired to do a job, and that job is not excursioner."

"He tried to kill your partner and threatened all those innocent people." Desi's tone had a note of finality, as though nothing Lavon could or would say would remotely challenge his conclusion.

Lavon put down his fork and looked at Desi like they were the only people in the room. "Son, when I first became a lawman, my father sat me down and had a long talk with me. He told me about lawmen who, with the best of intentions, let their personal anger and views overshadow their judgment. Many of these lawmen overstepped the guidelines of law. My father told me that criminals don't bring criminals to justice; lawmen do."

"Sean and I have been discussing creating a new position. Director of City Operation. That person would be over the Police, Fire department, and Public Works. Those departments would still have their chief, but those chiefs would report to that director." The mayor introjected.

"Sounds like someone with your core values might consider throwing his hat in the ring over," Hardcastle added.

"Wait a minute, my mother, Mildred Lance, has supported the city long before this guy showed up." Desi defended.

"No one is removing anyone from their current positions. But projects are underway that will expand Shepherds Pass, and we need to be clear about the future. Besides, if Mildred feels the job should be hers, she can apply." Hardcastle noted.

"I hope it works out, but I am not interested in applying now." Lavon smiled.

"If you are concerned about being separated from that Blackwell woman, I am sure you could find something at double her current salary working beneath you."

There was something in the expression beneath you coming from Clara that made Lynn's blood boil to the point of speechlessness.

"THERE YOU ARE." LYNN located Lavon in his room at the mansion. Lavon had been given his own space in the mansion but never spent the night in that room. He had always slept in bed with Lynn. When a friend's girlfriend was missing, and Lavon had overseen locating her, Lavon had grown an acute sensitivity to what it would be like to have the person you love the most out there somewhere and not to be able to reach them. Lavon was sitting on the edge of the bed, and when Lynn came in, he shoved something into an old, tattered duffle bag. Lynn had dressed for bed and was carrying a snifter of the gifted brandy. "What are you hiding, Porn."

"It's an old friend." Lavon reached into the bag and retrieved the old leather-bound bible that looked like it had been through a war.

"Are we a couple?"

"Yes."

"Then is there ever a time when you will say, I don't know, let us talk it over?"

"You are upset about my turning down a position too good to be true."

"I am a little upset that you would not even consider it. I have dedicated my life to fixing this mess, and you could have been able to do a lot of good."

"I knew the offer was coming."

"What, how could you?"

"Someone told me. They told me it is a trap."

"So, you were relying on your old friend there to help you make the right choices."

"When it is time for a Tyler child to leave home, my momma gives them bible like this. She says you don't have to read it, and you don't have to even look at it. But everywhere you travel, take it with you.

That way, since it is a gift from me, it is like you are taking a small piece of me with you wherever you go.

This old friend went with me to college, where I had to hide it to keep people from thinking I was a religious freak. Then it went with me into military service, and I found out that I was not alone in depending on this type of friend in combat." Lavon paused and looked at Lynn, now seeing her vulnerabilities shining through.

"Tell me about the bad dreams."

Lynn hesitated and fortified herself with a stiff drink of brandy. "It's about my mother. We don't get along the way we should. In the dream, I am hiding from her, but she keeps finding me."

"And what does this have to do with Paden?"

"Paden has played referee in the past. You see, it all seems so unfair. My Aunt and Rosa, the maid, raised me; motherhood never took for my mother. I watched your mother when I went to the family event with you and your family. There were over fifty little kids, and she walked up to each of them individually and talked to them about the last time they spoke. When you were unconscious in the hospital, I talked to your mother, and I thought it was my job to comfort her, but she was comforting me."

Lynn was now crying. "How could that horrible woman offer Abby as a paid mistress beneath you in my face."

For the remainder of the night embraced and consoled each other as they prepared for what lie ahead. That which could not be foretold.

Chapter 9

Lavon and Abby walked into the Lyondell Coffee Shop, suspicious of why they were there.

Abby had gotten an early morning call from Barney, and he wanted to meet with her and Lavon. Barney's instructions added the texture of mystery to the rendezvous. No one but she and Lavon. They were kept from telling where they were going or who they were meeting. If they felt they were being followed, abort the meeting.

"I am starting to feel like a spy. Why do you make me feel like a spy, Mr. Tyler?" Abby complained.

"I don't know, but there in the corner is Bud Stagwell."

"Who?"

"The missing bodyguard and he is seated with your friend Barney." Lavon led the way. "This seems like a promising meeting."

"How did you find this guy?" Abby asked, seating herself.

"You might say Bud here found me." Barney slurped his coffee and took a big bite of a Danish. "You see, Bud had one of my street contacts call me and set up a meeting. The meet requires that I bring Detective Tyler."

Bud was as big as his coworker, who had been found recently with a bullet hole in his head. Bud looked like a middle-aged actor who could still send women rushing to the box office to see whatever garbage of a movie he might be in.

"Do we know each other, sir?" Lavon asked, shaking the man's hand, and being seated.

"No. But I am a former cop. Baltimore PD. And I do my research."

"Former cop. Did you get caught with your hand in the cookie jar?" Abby mocked.

"No, I got caught with evidence stolen for the police lock up that freed a known low life and gangster."

"Let me guess, you were set up." Abby shot back.

"Since you guys may have to take what I say at face value, why don't I give you the redacted version of my resume? I did not even know who the gangster was. A cop set me up because I was sleeping with his wife."

"Did you sing this sad story for the internal affairs officers?" Abby asked.

"Yeah. I came clean to them. The only problem was there was more than one cop's wife who enjoyed my company. So, I was never sure which one set me up.

Internal affairs told me to resign, and there would be no further investigation."

"How did you come to work for Dodd?" Lavon asked.

"That's the funny part. I tried cop jobs everywhere, but word was circulating that I was dirty and worked for mobsters."

"So, you are a pig whose deep dick dives in his buddy's wives, but you want us to believe anything you tell us is the truth."

"Look, lady?"

"Detective Blackwell." Abby corrected.

"Well, Detective Blackwell, I don't know if the bug has ever bitten you to sleep around, but it is a tough master. Somewhere along the road, I may have lost my soul or the right for you to listen to me, but I had to tell you guys you are in trouble, and someone wants to kill you, and it aint Dolan Dodd."

Abby looked to Lavon to catch the sinking feeling Bud had imposed on her with a shot to the heart by mentioning the sleeping around fixation.

"How do you know it aint Dolan," Barney asked between bites.

"Dolan issued an order no one from any organized family is to touch a hair on the head of Lavon Tyler."

"Why," Abby questioned.

"Dolan gives orders. He doesn't explain order."

"What can you tell me about Walter?" Lavon thought he would test the waters.

"All I know about the guy you arrested at the hospital is that he was hired by the guy your partner killer. It wouldn't surprise me if the guy had no clue what any of this mess is about. But just because you have a hall pass from Dolan doesn't mean your partner does."

"Bud, do me a favor and put on your cop thinking cap momentarily. Do you think the shootout at Abby's and the attempted murder of Dolan are related?"

"My instincts say yes, but I also fear people that use disposable hit men. They can lead a ghost trail that isn't real."

"Did you notice anything different about the other bodyguard, Rinehart Sheldon?"

"As a cop, you keep thinking about what I missed when things go ape shit. I missed that he was getting calls from a woman recently."

"Was he gay?" Abby asked.

"No, just the opposite, he, shall we say love only sections of a woman.

Prostitutes were his style. I was surprised a pussy other than Prudence held his attention."

"Was Prudence a lover?" Lavon asked.

"Not that type of pussy. Prudence was a kitten someone gave him."

The rest of the conversation was minor details. Bud knew little that would help them. He only wanted to be able to hide out until

whatever was happening had blown over. Bud felt that if the cops kept
looking for him, they would find him leaving a trail that would mean
his demise.

"So, I thought you were working with O'Leary?" Abby noted after
they allowed Bud to find a place to hide out.

"Well, this may come as a shock to you, but I aint as young as I used
to be.

If I brought O'Leary the next thing, we know he and your partner
are duking it out. And you don't have the energy to break it up? I save
that type of energy for the wife of forty years, so she doesn't go, as you
say, find some stud to do some deep dick diving on my ranch."

"LAVON, HAVE YOU EVER met my wife?" Lavon was at his desk
reading some information he had requested based on his conversations
with Walter and now with Bud. Don Nash posed the question, and
Lavon looked up, unaware that Abby had left the chair.

"No. Can't say that I have."

"She is homely."

"I beg your pardon." Lavon was sure he had misheard the new
Lieutenant.

"I don't mean that in a spiteful or mean way."

"I see." But Lavon did not; he only put the papers away to find out
what the conversation was supposed to be about.

"I met her in church years ago, and she was even homelier then. I
went out on a date with her to satisfy both our families. One day, she
realized she loved me."

"All's ways well, that ends well, I suppose."

"We have four girls. All with drastic overbite issues."

"Oh." Lavon could barely reframe from laughing. If this was a joke,
had they reached the part that was supposed to be funny?

"They look like a batch of beavers, all but the youngest; she looks like a little woodchuck."

"Lieutenant, where are we going with this?"

"Well, the way I see it, it will cost me a fortune in dental work to get those girls married off. My wife wants to have another child. She says the odds are it would be the son I always wanted. I didn't have the heart to tell her odd don't work that way, and I don't want a son bad enough to risk it."

"I will admit, I am lost."

"Let me help you find your way. I need my job. When I heard Lieutenant Crawford was being promoted, I figured that was why she brought you in."

"Don, I am not out to steal your job."

"I know something is going on around here. And someone sent that Ivy guy to look over my shoulder."

"I don't really know him."

"Funny to hear you say that because he reminds me a lot of you. He is brilliant. He showed up out of nowhere a few years back, and now he is riding high in the command structure."

Abby returned. "Dispatch just got a call that someone tried to shoot the mayor."

"How is he?" Nash asked.

"They missed him, but Hardcastle is being rushed to the emergency room.

He took two rounds from a high-power rifle." Abby answered, handing Lavon his jacket.

"Damn." Was the only thing Nash could say as he watched most of the police squad room evacuate.

Chapter 10

The crime scene took up most of the remainder of the evening. Someone had shot Sean Hardcastle at a breakout session from a meeting. Sean and the Mayor had been having coffee in an outdoor area of the court grounds.

Three shots were fired. Two hit Hardcastle, and a third hit a deputy assigned to the courts who heard the shots and rushed toward the mayor to pull him away from the line of fire. The deputy, having sustained a head wound and massive blood loss, died on the spot.

"Two in the center ring," Abby whispered to Lavon, trying to be sure the other detective officers and technicians did not hear.

"That bothers me too. The first two shots were in Hardcastle. What do you say while everyone is trying to figure out who wanted the mayor dead? We concentrate on who wants to kill Hardcastle."

"The shorter list would be who doesn't. The man is a weasel responsible for the hard feeling between all the public agencies and the local news media." Abby paused, then asked. "Did your brother go home?"

"No, he was going to go back, but Paden has been staying at the house, and he writes songs when depressed. She has been singing the duet parts."

"Do you think they are becoming an item?"

"I think she likes him from the way I see her watch him when he plays the guitar or keyboards. He agreed to play a set at her restaurant tonight. But the truth is, he still thinks he can work it out with Shavon.

"So, you are saying he is a true romantic, and the sad country songs are his outlet?"

"No, I think you had it right the first day you met him. Cute as the dickens but dumb as a box of rocks."

Chapter 11

"Lovester, I am still shaking. That is the most nervous I have ever been. I thought just because I played tennis in front of a crowd of people." Paden was shaken after the performance she Lovester had done at Paden's Place.

The crowd went wild, listening to them perform together. The original music captivated the audience and held them as if they were watching a play unfold.

"I had better get my brother's jacket back to his room before he gets home." Lovester had borrowed a jacket and county hat from Lavon for pictures to be taken with the guest and later hung on the wall of the restaurant. Lovester helped Paden from the car as they parked in the driveway of the mansion.

"When are you leaving for home?" Paden said in a voice she hoped did not reveal her desire to have him stay longer.

"I feel so lost in a big city like this."

"You miss her, don't you? The girl that broke your heart."

"I wish I could be like those guys that can jump from one woman to another. I keep asking myself what I could have done differently."

"Hey, Tyler." A voice called out. Three men had been hidden in the shadow and now made themselves known. Lovester turned to face the man who called his name, and a shot rang out. Lovester spread his arms to shield Paden, and there was another shot. Paden screamed, and the men walked closer. All the men carried guns. One man pointed his gun at Paden's face.

"Oh shit, that aint him." The second man stumbles to reveal.

"What?" The third man asked.

"That aint Lavon Tyler; looks a lot like him, but up close, you can see this kid is younger."

The first man still had his gun pointed toward Paden's face, and suddenly, there was recognition in his eyes. "Jesus Christ, this is Constantine Dodds, kid." The man started shaking as an angry fire began to burn in Paden's eyes.

"Pull the trigger. Pull the goddamn trigger; that's the only way you assholes have a fighting chance of staying alive." Paden could see the fear rooted in the eyes of the men. Paden slapped the gun away and kneeled to apply pressure to Lovester.

"Hold on, baby. Please, for me, hold on."

Chapter 12

"**I** can't explain how good it felt pulling the trigger," Desi confessed to his mother. They were in her office at the Department of Public Works. Mildred hugged her son with great pride. "I only wish I had shot the man that raped you, mother."

"His time is coming, and now he knows to live in fear. He can no longer be protected by the balance of power in Shepherds Pass."

"What does the benefactor say about our progress?"

"He is pleased beyond belief. Even if Dolan is not dead, all eyes are starting to focus on the mayor and his side of the clan. A war between the two sides of the Dodd family is inevitable. The only thing that can stop that is Lavon Tyler's remaining neutral. But the benefactor says he will deal with Tyler."

"I met Tyler. He sounds like an uneducated hick."

Mildred smiled at her son's quickness to adopt prejudice as fact. "No, Desi, he is quite educated and a smart cop. He uses the weakness covertly hiding in our underestimating him to collect information from us without our knowing it."

"How do you know so much about him?"

"By examining the mistakes of Amber Dodd."

LAVON HAD BEGUN SEARCHING for information on Mildred and Desi Lance. Lavon knew he would have to perform at least a cursory interview with them, and it would be best to sound like he knew a little about them. Immediately, he noticed something was wrong. Mildred had degrees in accounting and mathematics but no engineering background, which was a red flag for someone who oversaw public works. The only job Desi had held was at the Department of Public Works, and he had started in a midlevel position, not an intern or even a starting position.

Dodd family employment placing at work, he thought. So why did Desi seem so upset that he was not qualified for the job that might be created? In the notation, there was a reference to a file in Mildred's information. The file number had a police code. When Lavon attempted to access another system to see what the file was regarding, he got an error message stating that the information he was requesting was no longer system accessible. Lavon thought since this was a new building with a new system, everything in it that was moved here from the old building should be accessible. Lavon wanted to let it go, but he could not. He got up, went to records, and pulled the hard copy associated with the file number he found. In the folder was blank typing paper.

When Lavon returned from the record room, Abby was reading the incoming memos. He dropped the Mildred Lance folder in front of her.

"Okay, I'll bite; what's wrong?"

"That is the Mildred Lance, formally Mildred Hardcastle folder."

Abby opened the folder and thumbed through the blank pages. "Not very wordy, is it?" She smirked. "So, what is supposed to be in here?"

"Who knows, maybe she is an Alien or crawled up out of the sea, but someone went through the trouble of investigating and then replaced the file."

"Replaced?"

"Yes, dear. You see, if they had just not done the work, why create a case number?"

Suddenly, the gravity of the problem hit Abby. "Someone had to remove the file and replace it with blank paper, so there was no jump in the numbering. What does the computer say it was?"

"The computer says it expired and is no longer in the system."

"That's not right."

"It sounds like someone created a dead end that we can't get past."

"Not necessarily. Handwritten field notes are in boxes in the basement. If you promise to spring for the allergy medicine, we can look up the corresponding date, day, and number. The cop that answered the original call will have his name on the notes."

"ZEB GUNDERSON RETIRED," Abby shouted like she had struck gold after hours of digging through boxes that led to dead ends.

"There you two are," Webber exclaimed, locating Lavon and Abby. Webber rushed over and hugged Lavon.

"Okay, what did I miss?" Abby asked, letting out a big sneeze.

"There are cars at the mansion where you live. There has been a shooting. The first responding officers thought it was you. They say he looks and dresses like you." Webber released Lavon, a little embarrassed about the emotional release.

"Lester," Abby shouted, but Lavon had already headed for the door.

Chapter 13

After a month of weather that averaged at least ten degrees higher than usual, Shepherds Pass received its payoff—a flash downpour. The cold rain hit the hot pavements and sent steam and humidity searing through the air. Mildred Lance sat in the back seat of the stretch limo with the man that was the benefactor of her plan to get even with the man that had raped her years ago.

He poured himself a drink and then offered Mildred one. Mildred declined. She did not know if she was comfortable in the presence of this man, but she knew his power, and it would be his power that would be needed to defeat her enemies.

"There is no need to fear me, Mildred. The work you and your son have done to ensure success in our mutual plan has more than exceeded my expectations."

Mildred sat facing the man, noticing the light created by the flashes of Saint Elmo's Fire in the distance. The light made him look almost handsome. He certainly did not look like the mobster she knew him to be. "Thank you."

"No thank you is required. You have done well. And you ask so little of my part in the plan."

"I know what I need to know to get my job done. But please let me ask one thing of you." Mildred requested.

Donavan Malone, the man smiling back at Mildred from the shadows of the limo, nodded for her to make her request. "I understand you lost over one hundred million dollars from the Robin Hood bandits here on Dolan Dodd's turf. And right under his nose with, him making no offer to reimburse you for your losses. But that is money, and how you handle that is your choice. I only ask when it comes time to kill the man who raped me and stole my life. That is when it becomes time to kill Mayor Dodd. You consider letting me pull the trigger."

"The women I have embraced since I was a teen have been women for hire. They have always had their agenda, as have had mine. I do not know, or will I ever understand, the mechanism that exists in a man's mind that would force himself on a woman that did not desire his touch. But that alone does not drive my earnestness to this task. I cannot abide a man who would deny his son and force that son into servitude for life. It makes me sick to my stomach."

Mildred thought this man was the opposite of what she expected. He was sympathetic in a way many men are not. He is even eloquent about his motives, no matter how harsh the means of achieving them might turn out to be.

LAVON BURST INTO THE emergency entrance of Shepherd Pass General Hospital in full stride. He did not seem to know or care that he was leaving Abby and Lopez to race to keep up with him. The scene at the hospital was different than the night he met Walter, the shooter that tried to kill Abby. The hospital looked as much like a police station substation as a place for the sick and injured. Lavon knew this was because Sean Hardcastle was a patient here.

"Tyler, over here." Lavon heard the commanding voice of Sergeant Rush. Sargent Rush was a muscular drill instructor type, a no-nonsense man who had worked with Lavon. Rush had no doubt seen Tyler's eyes panning the groups of people engaged in their misfortunes and maladies, trying to find some to lead him to Lovester. Rush turned and headed down a hallway without waiting for acknowledgment from

Lavon. Rush led to a space near a reception desk where Grey Wolf, Paden's bodyguard stood with two uniformed officers Lavon had not formally met. When Grey Wolf stepped aside, Lavon caught a glimpse of Paden. She was a different Paden that the one he had first observed, the returning tennis pro. She was also not the semi-flirty mobster's granddaughter he had met in the restaurant. At this moment in time, Paden seemed reduced to a frightened child. Paden's eyes were red and swollen as if she had cried every tear she could produce. Though once artistically applied, Paden's makeup was a complete mess caused by the tears and rain. She wore an oversized Shepherds Pass Police Department windbreaker, which meant her other wear was taken as evidence of a crime. Lavon knew Paden's clothes had no doubt been saturated with his brother's blood. A feeling overcame Lavon as he hugged Paden. He could feel what Lynn must have felt watching him hover at the gateway to death, not knowing if he would return to this world when he had been injured.

"It was all my fault, Uncle Lavon; I told Lovester to wear your jacket and hat for the singing engagement." Paden rushed free of the officers questioning her, and Grey Wolf, her protector then buried her face deeply in Lavon's chest.

"Who did this?" Was Lavon's first question.

"I don't know. There were three of them. One said, awh shit, that aint him he is too young."

"Detective Tyler, we need to get her to a sketch artist as soon as possible; she has refused to leave until you got here," Rush explained.

"You will have to go with them, Paden."

Paden looked at the circle of people that had started to gather around her and Lavon. Paden led Lavon slightly away to prevent everyone from hearing the next thing she had to say.

"He's going to make it. And when he does, please do not tell him what a mess I was. Don't let him know." The revelation she was about to make froze in her throat.

"That you are starting to like him a lot." Lavon finished her statement.

"I think I fell in love with him on stage in mid-song. Then I had to realize the girl he is really singing about and writing those heartfelt songs about is some bitch named Shavon."

"Go with the cops and be here when he wakes up."

"YOU ARE TALLER THAN I remember." A female East Indian doctor approached Lavon as he led Paden back to Grey Wolf and the police.

"Have we met?" Lavon asked, confused.

"I worked on you the night you were admitted for that double beating you took."

"Now I remember. You are the doctor that shot me full of those drugs that had me doing a spirit walk."

Grey Wolf smiled, being perhaps the only one who understood the joke.

"At first, I thought it was you again."

"He's one of my younger brothers."

"Well, this is his second surgery, and we are trying to build his strength and assess where we go from here; I am Doctor Patel, just in case you did not recall."

AS SOON AS THE UNIFORMED officers led Paden out of site, Sergeant Rush turned to Lavon. "Detective, you are with me." Rush held his hand like a crossing guard for Abby and Lopez to remain where they were and not follow. Rush led Lavon down a long hall to what looked like a service elevator. The two men entered the elevator, and Rush pressed the sub-basement level button. When the elevator reached the lowest level, Rush pointed straight forward, and Lavon exited the elevator. Rush made no further statements, but it was clear whatever Lavon had been invited to did not interest or concern him. The elevator closed, and Rush was gone. The room smelled of strong formaldehyde. Gurneys were covered in white linen, clearly the remains of lost hope and incomplete dreams and the vessels that once carried them.

Lavon strode forward, and out from behind a corner stepped Police Deputy Director Dana Crawford. Dana Crawford had brought Lavon to Shepherds Pass to assist the suffering detective department. Director Crawford was a friend of Lavon's father, and many suspected the relationship had exceeded the boundaries of general friendship at some point in the past. From behind her stepped Detective Ivy.

"Considering all the trouble this cloak and dagger business is, I should be hurt. You don't seem the slightest bit surprised." Ivy confessed.

"My only surprise is that it took my brother being shot for you two to bring me in." Lavon ignored Ivy and stared directly at Crawford.

"I won't apologize for what I have done. I have always been a friend to you and your father, and nothing has changed. I am sorry Lovester got caught in the crossfire."

"Sorry. That sounds good and fixes that. Now, let's talk about a couple of other things. Intelligence would have known that Dolan Dodd put out a no hit order me. The only way to slow me down then would be to knock the legs from under me by putting a hit on my partner."

"Look, that one is on me," Ivy confessed.

"She has fucked up in the past, and maybe in some ways she still does, but she is not expendable." Lavon now looked at Ivy.

"Look, you are police chief's son; you know how intel works. I got the news too late to verify and act."

"For the record, my brother is not just another piece of a chess game. He aint no pawn to be sacrificed. And just so you know, Dolan Dodd had nothing to do with shooting my brother."

"Boys don't fight. We have too many problems to squabble among ourselves." Dana took both men by the hand. "I sent Detective Ivy over because I did not feel good about moving up with so much unresolved conflict landing on Nash's plate."

"Balance of power? What was Amber Dodd talking about?" Lavon asked, then noticed the shocked stare on Dana and Ivy's faces. "If you are trying to decide how much to tell me, considering people are dying, all would be a good place to start."

Dana nodded, giving Ivy permission to begin the explanation. "In a very short time, the Football League is expected to rule on adding three new teams to the league in new cities. One is to cover a team that wants to leave where it is because of a dwindling market. The other two will be in new cities, and Shepherd Pass is on the shortlist. That would mean billions of dollars in expansion and job growth."

"So far, we have been tasked with balancing the power of the mayor's family and Dolan's group equally. And no one has crossed the line until the night of the awards dinner." Dana added.

"The third power," Lavon stated.

"What?" Ivy looked shocked.

"Look at the events. Someone tries to kill Dolan and start a war between the two sides of the family. That would mean his son comes home, who, as I am told, hates politicians with a passion. There is a no-kill order on me, but someone tries to kill me to make the offshore gangster guy mad and pull them in. That Nicky Braden and his band of decapitators show up."

"Wait, you talked to Braden?" Ivy asked, astonished.

"How is the ownership split supposed to work?" Lavon asked.

"One-third to both sides of the family and a third to the city."

LYNN SAT BY HERSELF on a sofa in the waiting room near where Lovester was recovering. She sat staring at the cell phone in her hand. Lynn had just spoken to Lavon's mother and father and waited for Lavon to return from wherever he had wandered off. Nya sat down beside Lynn and took her hand.

"No offense, Nya, but I don't believe in fortune-telling."

"Do you believe in friendship?"

"Yes."

"Then there is no harm in us talking, is there?"

"I have been so mean to him lately. I have been closed off to him. He doesn't deserve it."

"So, what is the problem?"

"How do you deal with it? Every day, I send him off to the arms of a woman I know loves him?"

"I don't know Abby that well, and I am sure I do not know whether she is capable of love. But I do offer you something to think about. One of Wendell's best friends is Webber."

"She is gay."

"So, in my mind, I used to think that every morning when she got out of bed, she had the same basic equipment I have."

"I think I see your point. Just never thought about it like that."

"I learned Wendell always wished he had a younger brother or sister. In some way, Webber fills both those slots. I love him too much to deny him that."

"So, are you telling me to be a big girl and stop complaining?"

"I am telling you to be a cop's wife. I had to first learn how to be a cop's wife." With this, Nya sashayed off.

Chapter 14

"Have you heard anything on how your brother is doing?" Abby asked. She and Lavon were at Zeb's Magic Touch. Zeb's Magic Touch was a beauty salon owned by Zeb Gunderson, the retired detective whose name appeared on the missing file folder with Mildred Lance's name. Zeb and a young woman, clearly his granddaughter, worked in a room full of women, the youngest in her late seventies. Zeb was a man who looked like he had once been big and strong, but his midsection was canceling out his completely athletic build. Zeb wore a cheap hairpiece and false teeth that looked like they were two sizes too large for his mouth.

"One of my sisters is coming up to sit with him. My father said that I must get off my ass and find the bastards that did that to him."

Zeb took the time to flirt with his entire elderly clientele individually.

"I see old pimps never die," Abby whispered to Lavon.

Finally, it was Lavon and Abby's turn for attention. "Well, she is far too beautiful to need my magic, if I may say," Zeb stated, reaching to touch Abby's dark shoulder-length curly. Abby smacked his hand.

"We are here to talk about the empty folder you left in the police station when you retired."

"How many?"

"How many what?" Lavon asked.

"Well, I guess you two are from Hollywood, and this is finally my big chance. So how many million are we talking about."

"Look, old guy, we are cops. Do you remember cops? You used to be one. We lock people up for stealing what does not belong to them. "Abby explained.

Zeb smiled at the threat. "Well, congratulations. For going on twenty-five years, people have walked past the empty folder. It has been shuffled and moved from room to room and building to building. The folder has come up in internal audits, and the number being correct on the outside of the folder is the only thing those pinheads found to be interesting. Now you two had the intelligence to open the file and find it contained blank paper."

"Zeb, if I must confess, most days I am usually the more reasonable of the two of us, but someone shot my brother, and I think it has something to do with whatever was in that folder. So, what I am going to do is drag you out back and beat you until I feel better." Lavon started to stand up.

"Hold on, I will tell you what was in that folder. I just thought you two were here to make a movie about it. Rape."

"Start from the beginning." Lavon and Abby moved closer so the clients could not hear.

"I got a call that there was a rape at a hotel downtown after some political shindig, and the girl was beaten up really bad. I got to the hotel, and the uniform cops were shaking in their boots when they found out how the perp was."

"Hardcastle?" Abby guessed.

"No sugar, it was the Honorable Mayor Dodd. Of course, he wasn't mayor back then; his father was."

"Two weeks later, this girl comes in and changes her statement and drops all charges. She then said it was her boyfriend. She was mad at him and filed a false report to piss him off. The boyfriend she named was Sean Hardcastle."

"You knew something was wrong with the story that is why you substituted the file," Abby asked.

"Look, I have been a cop since before either of you was an itch in your pappy's pants. I know horse shit when I hear it. Hardcastle was in D.C. that night on business in front of fifty prominent people. Now, two weeks later, she marries Hardcastle. Seven months later, Junior is born. And a year later, they divorce."

"What happens to the file?" Lavon asked.

"Kid, you got wax in your ears. I still got the file."

Chapter 15

"The Shepherds Pass Department of Public Works building was an engineering marvel, just not in a good way. The building looked like it had been built and furnished by robots for other robots, that the first group of robots did not like. The floors were covered in a tile that looked like it could last for centuries. The guest chairs gave you back pain just from looking at them. And on the walls, in place of pictures or art, were maps, diagrams, and blueprints. The cooling system kept the room cold, but it did not account for the stern look on the faces of all the employees. There was piped-in overhead music resembling elevator music but did not quite meet that standard.

"This must be hell." Abby proclaimed.

Mildred sat staring at Lavon with no expression on her face for moments that seemed like an hour. "Let me guess, you reconsidered the mayor's offer and are taking the job. Now you want me out so you can install your concubine." Mildred finally spoke, then rolled his eyes toward Abby.

"Does that word mean what I think it means?" Abby leaned toward Lavon.

"It actually means wife of a lesser stature. In systems with multiple wives, sometimes the wives have ranks. But I do think she meant to say what you are thinking." Lavon answered.

"Bravo, I told my son not to be fooled by that country hick accent."

"Mrs. Lance, we only stopped by to ask about your ex-husband. It is typical when such a person is shot." Lavon explained.

"The man is a rodent. And you don't like him any more than I do."

"Did you shoot him?" Abby asked.

"No. Did you?" Mildred's level of agitation was getting higher and higher. Mildred was unaware this was what Abby wanted.

"So, let's talk about the mayor," Abby stated.

"What about the mayor." Mildred was now shaking with fury.

"His hands. His touch. His hot breath on your neck."

Mildred vaulted over the desk and lunged at Abby, knocking her backward. Abby had Mildred in handcuffs in seconds.

"That was a pretty dirty trick," Lavon told Abby as they watched the uniformed cops, they called haul Mildred away.

"Just mad because you didn't think of it first. And what is this shit that you turned down a six-figure job, and the only thing I got to do is sex you up when Lynn is worn out?"

"We can discuss that later. Let's just hope the second part of this stupid plan works."

"WHAT THE HELL ARE YOU doing." Noreen Tyler screamed while entering her brother's hospital room. Noreen Tyler is the sister of Lavon and Lovester Tyler. Noreen recently graduated law school passed the bar exam, and now works as an intern in St. Louis. Noreen is smaller in stature than many of her thirteen brothers and sisters, but Noreen was known to have the heart of a lion when needed and, more importantly, the heart of a Tyler woman.

"I need him to sign these papers, or I might lose my trailer and all my stuff. The sheriff put a padlock on it." Shavon replied, attempting to look pitiful.

"I told her he can't sign anything; he is still unconscious." A duty nurse, a frail red-headed girl who had been trying to block Shavon from touching Lovester, cried out. "I need to get security, but procedure says I can't leave him in the room along with a madwoman."

"Look bitch watch that madwoman shit." Shavon snapped. Shavon was Lovester's former fiancée. They had recently broken up. Shavon told Lovester it was because she had had an illicit affair with his brother Lavon. The truth was that it was Shavon who had been unfaithful to Lovester, and Lavon knew about it because his former fiancée had also been unfaith during the same party. Lovester gave Shavon a time limit to tell his brother the truth, or the next time he saw his brother, he would reveal the truth. That made Shavon fabricate the story that sent Lovester to Shepherds Pass to confront his brother.

"Shavon, it's a contact. The first thing about any contract is being of sound mind and body. Does my brother look like he is of sound mind and body to you? Stop being selfish. He is fighting for his life right now."

"Just like you, Noreen. Never thinking about anyone else but your precious family. Well, others have to live, too. And what if he dies?"

Both the question and the image it projected in Noreen's mind propelled her across the room, forcing her to shove Shavon backward. Shavon bounced off the nurse, and the nurse hit the floor.

"What the fuck are you people doing?" A woman's voice came from the doorway. It was Paden Dodd.

"Just who the hell are you." Shavon shrieked.

"I am Lovester's friend and singing partner. Paden. We were together the night he was shot."

"Oh, it's all clear now. Lavon goes and finds himself some uptown tail and now he has his brother dump me up for a trade-up."

"I am Noreen, his sister. And Shavon, I think you need to leave." Noreen stated, grabbing Shavon by the arm. Shavon pulled away and punched Noreen in the eye. This was the same eye Noreen had been punched in by a jealous woman over a man recently. Paden spun Shavon around and hit her in the midsection with a left, followed by a right to the jaw. The nurse crawled from beneath the pile of falling women and out the door. Two security guards return to corral the women. Lovester slept soundly through the entire ordeal.

"SO, TELL ME AGAIN WHY you need this?" Ivy asked. Ivy stood in Lavon and Abby sat listening.

"We need to know who the law firm is that released Mildred Lance that is the connection to the out-of-town gangsters trying to muscle in," Lavon answered.

"So, you are saying Mildred shot her ex-husband, Hardcastle?" Ivy checked.

"No. Desi belongs to a gun club and is a marksman. He shot Hardcastle." Abby explained.

"So, Desi shot his father, why?"

"Hardcastle is no more Desi's father than I am," Abby answered.

"I was right. It would take O'Leary years to figure this stuff out."

"Remember that the next time you hold a spy meeting in a morgue. I should have been invited. Besides, I read that overexposure to formaldehyde can cause swelling of the testicles." Abby noted.

"Should I step away so you can examine your partner?" Ivy asked.

"No need. I had mine checked last night. They are doing just fine." Lavon answered.

A receptionist leaned over Ivy's shoulder. "They want one of you upstairs; they got a couple of women brawling at the hospital."

"So," Lavon responded.

"So, one says she is your niece, and one says she is your sister."

"Can I handle this? It is time for me and Paden to clear the air. This making amends stuff sucks," Abby requested.

"It's all yours." Lavon agreed.

"The third woman is in a holding cell downstairs." The receptionist noted.

"Who is she?" Lavon noticed the startled look on Abby's face.

"Shavon."

"Good luck. And by the way, is the sister's name is it, Jody?" Lavon asked.

"No, Noreen. Don't you know your own sister's name?" The receptionist asked.

"When he was a kid, his old lady lived in a shoe," Abby answered and was off.

PADEN AND NOREEN SAT in the office, not saying anything for a while. Finally, the silence got to Paden. "Why do you suppose they put us in an office rather than putting us in a cell?"

"Because I am an officer of the court, and they don't want to start that process unless there is no other way."

"You're a cop?"

"No, a lawyer. And it still sounds funny to hear myself say it."

"Are you the sister he calls Little Bit? Uncle Lovester, I mean."

"Yeah, how did you know?"

"He has slipped a few times and called me that. I think I remind him of you."

"We are about the same height, but you are so much more well-developed."

They were quiet again for a moment, and the question Paden had to ask came out. "When the men came toward us shooting, Lovester didn't duck or even flinch. He opened his arms to shield me from being shot. What kind of guy does that for a girl he barely knows?" The glaze of tears was trying to sneak out in Paden's eyes.

"A Tyler man."

"I KNOW THERE IS BAD blood between us. And I accept that it is my fault. I stood the and watched that cop feel you up, and I didn't do a damn thing. I hate that it happened. Right now, I am trying to amend some of the bad shit I did in the past. That night stands out in my mind more than any other. I am not asking you to forgive me, and I am not asking that you just try to understand. I don't want my fuck ups to taint how you carry yourself or feel about yourself." Abby had located Noreen and Paden and the venom in Paden eyes showed when Abby entered the room.

"Lady, I will forgive you a million times over if you can get me out of here. I don't want Lovester to wake up alone. Please"

"WELL, SHAVON, I MUST say it is wonderful seeing you again." Abby began. A large female guard led Shavon into an interview room. Shavon was in handcuffs.

"Take her cuffs off."

The guard removed the handcuffs. "Well, that's more like it." Shavon began rubbing her wrists.

"Please sign this." Abby laid a pen and some forms in front of Shavon.

"What is that for."

"It is dismissing the current charges as a cross-complaint between you and the girls you had the altercation with."

Shavon signed the papers. "Good, now can I go?"

"Turn around."

"What for?"

"Well, Shavon, I am re-arresting you on a capias warrant. Seems a judge requested to speak with you about the exploding Lexus and the driver, but you did not show up."

"My lawyer was supposed to handle that."

"Only when you pay them."

"Oh, now I see what this is. Lavon has been putting his hand up your skirt, too."

"No, idiot. I tried, but he wasn't having it. My problem is that I walked your happy ass out of here, telling you that you had to return when requested. Now, my creditability is on the line. A hillbilly slut like you just isn't worth ruining my standing with judges I have to work with every day."

LAVON SAW A HEAD IN his pickup truck as he walked through the police garage. He thought it must be Noreen. Lavon had loaned his vehicle to his sister when she did not have reliable transportation so she would not miss school. He thought she must have kept a copy of the key somehow.

"Get in and close the door." It was Paden.

"So, if you are going to start breaking into cars, I have a tip. Don't do it in police garages."

"Look, smart ass, I did not break anything. I am meeting your sister at the hospital. She is going to tell me the story of Lynn visiting Lamont, Mississippi. But we need to talk first."

"So, talk."

"If you go to the bus station tonight just before midnight, you will see the three men who shot your brother."

"How?" Lavon needed help to formulate the question.

"Don't ask. And I cannot be asked to testify or to identify them, but they will be there. My father or grandfather cannot know that I told you. If my grandfather gets to them first, he has to eliminate them for operating on his tuff without permission." Paden spoke, looking down as if she memorized what she was going to say. "And one other thing. Noreen and I talked, and it's alright if we share the nickname Little Bit. So don't feel bad when you let that slip."

Lavon rested his head back and descended into thought. He noticed Paden was gone before realizing how long he had been thinking. Lavon sat for a moment, letting his mind adjust. Maybe this is what true friendship is. Being the best possible friend, you can be to the person you call your friend. And it had to be based on the version of you that you currently were. He knew little about Abby's past, but by her own admission, she was horrible and did bad things to people. Paden and Lovester barely knew each other, but they showed signs of friendship another might overlook. One day, Paden might be a mobster herself; she was surely learning the family craft. But one day, she might also be the happy restauranter who insisted he stuff himself with gourmet smoked food. For now, Paden was a friend and, more importantly, a friend to Lovester. On this and this alone, he would act.

LAVON ENTERED THE BUS station with Webber walking to his right. Lavon had spent much time arguing with Abby, explaining it was not a good idea for her to enter with him. Lavon thought they might be too easily spotted if the shooters knew what they looked like. Lavon wanted to reduce the risk of a second gunfight in less than a week in a heavily populated place. Lavon and Webber began eliminating possible. Wrong gender or groups too large for what they were looking for. Lavon had informed Sergeant Rush that he was in the area looking for a suspect. Lavon then suggested that they have cars respond as quickly as possible if called. The people he was hunting were stone-cold killers.

Webber tapped the tip of her nose with her fingertip to signal that she may have spotted a good match. Lavon walked past Webber like he did not know her toward the men she saw. Three men were standing closely in a heated discussion. The man in the middle looked and saw Lavon, and it was what Lavon was looking for—instant recognition. The man reached into his jacket and pulled out a gun, but before he could clear the gun, Webber fired a taser and shocked the man. The shocked man stood twitching, drooling, and peeing on himself, trying not to hit the ground. The two accomplices went for their guns, but Wendell tackled them on the left and Abby on the right; the bad guys went down so fast their heads collided before they smacked into the floor.

"Great work, guys. Now let's see if we can match the bullets from those guns to the ones from my brother." Lavon cheered.

"I think I like it when I don't get shot," Webber informed while helping with the handcuffing.

Chapter 16

Lavon entered the squad room a little later than usual. He had stopped to check on his brother. Lovester was doing better but still weak from the multiple surgeries. Paden was asleep with her arm across his chest, and Noreen was sleeping in a chair.

"I guess when you are as good as you two, you can come in whenever you want." It was the sound of Agent Patterson that had caught Lavon coming into his cubicle. Abby was already working. "You know a funny thing. I got a call early this morning from the deputy director of the FBI. You will never guess what he told me."

"If we guess, will you let us work?" Abby asked.

"He said some hot shots in your area arrested three of Donavan Malone's thugs last night."

"He makes this guessing thing easier than it should be," Abby commented, looking at Lavon.

Lavon ignored it, knowing what was coming.

"I told him that had to be a mistake because Malone is an east coast operator with no known rights to operate this far inland. He says you should check with Detectives Lavon Tyler and Abby Blackwell and their team of secret police.

"We matched one of the guns to shooting Lester," Abby stated. That is attempted murder and our problem.

"She missed my point." Patterson sat in the guest chair and put his head in his hands. "If you know a major East Coast hood was operating here, why didn't you tell me? And unless I missed something in FBI school, sending out a group of thugs to shoot someone is operating."

"You know you are starting to get those worry lines. Would you like to borrow some of my new moisturizers?"

"I heard Hardcastle died this morning. That bumps it up to murder. Shouldn't you guys find out who shot him?"

"We know who shot him?" Lavon stated, accepting a small box from the receptionist as she passed by.

"But you haven't arrested him."

"No rush. We are hoping he leads us to the rifle."

Abby began examining the small box and a diamond necklace fell from the box. Abby looked stunned. There was also matching earrings and a perfumed note card. Abby shook her head and dropped the box like it was hot. This caused Lavon to chuckle uncontrollably.

"It's from the little nutcase. There is a note that says there are matching panties if I would like to meet her somewhere to try them on." Abby looked horrified.

"How does it feel to be on the other side of the relentless flirting." Lavon asked as Patterson struggled to understand what was going on.

"Give that to Nash and have him lock it in a safe place until we can figure out what to do with it." Abby threw the box to Lavon.

"JUDGE ON THE FLOOR." A voice sounded. The alarm called out when a judge in robes appeared on the squad room floor. This was a rare occurrence and the first time Lavon had heard the warning.

"There you are." Lynn Dodd Masterson approached Lavon.

Judge Masterson appeared in full robe with Terrell, the court head bailiff assigned to keeping the judges safe. A crowd formed as all the detectives, uniform officers, and even suspects being questioned stopped to find out what was happening.

"Well, Judge, is there a problem?" Lavon asked as Abby stepped away.

"Well, yes, Detective Tyler, there is. I spoke to a friend, and now I know exactly what the problem is. I have been cranky and hard to get along with, and you keep doing everything you can to make me feel better. So, there is something I must do." Lynn winked at Terrell, and he took a pillow from behind his back and put it on the floor. "Stand up." Lynn commanded.

Lavon stood, and Lynn got down on one knee. Terrell handed her a box, and she removed a ring. "Lavon Tyler, will you marry me?"

The room cheered and broke out their phone cameras to capture the moment for posterity. Lavon was dazed.

"Hey, this is the part where you say yes," Terrell stated in his deep voice.

"Yes, oh yes."

Lynn slipped the ring on his finger.

"Now, dummy, you have to kiss her to make it official." Terrell instructed.

They kissed.

ABBY EXITED HER CAR in front of her apartment building, feeling confused. Lynn's proposal to Lavon had stirred feelings within her, and she was unsure how to accept them. Lynn's proposal meant that Lynn felt comfortable that the demons that drove Lavon to Shepherds Pass were under control. Abby knew that Lavon loved Lynn, but Abby knew there was a place in Lavon's heart for her. Friends, true friends, want what's best for each other.

Abby noticed a man and a woman in business suits walking toward her. Abby then saw two men standing in front of her building doorway, doing a poor job of looking like they were hanging around. Abby slid her hand to her service weapon. The man walking toward her opened the trench coat he wore over his suit and revealed a machine pistol on a strap underneath his arm.

"If you insist on a gunfight, lady, you will lose. The man only wants to talk to you. We promise it won't take long." The woman said in a throaty hiss.

A man Abby had not accounted for stepped out of the shadows, waved his hand, and a limo appeared. In a gentlemanly fashion, the man who had appeared opened the car door for Abby, took her hand to assist her into the car, and then closed the door.

"Yes, sir, I find that agreement more than satisfactory." A man in a tailored grey suit was finishing a phone call on a satellite phone. He sat circling something in the Wall Street Journal. "I have someone here that I need to speak to on that point, sir."

Abby sat impatiently in the seat facing the man, tapping her fingers on her knees.

"Abigail, I apologize for that; some last-minute information involving our conversation." He put away the phone. He then started to pour a drink from the limo bar. "Oh. I almost forgot." Then, put the liquor away.

"No, you didn't forget shit. You wanted me to know you know about my recovery. And that you have researched me." Abby leaned forward in a posture of defiance. "It is the type of lame ass shit dirtbag hoods do every day, and I am not impressed."

"Do you know who I am?"

"Yeah, you are Donovan Malone's East Coast hood." Abby continued to sit, staring directly at Donovan. "Now, here is one for you. Do you know you are sitting smack in the middle of Dolan Dodd's territory? And I don't know about you, but I don't want to spend the weekend hanging upside down in a meat locker trying to explain our little impromptu meeting. I suggest you drive around; preferably somewhere this ocean liner wouldn't stand out."

"Good point," Donovan commented and instructed the driver to drive near the airport the loopback.

"Your partner is very smart." Finally, Donovan spoke again. Donovan had been sizing Abby up in silence.

"Yeah, he is."

"Your partner anticipated this exact meeting. The only difference is that he is sitting right where you are in his version of the meeting. So please don't waste the opportunity with your sassy attitude, Abigail." Donovan took Abby's hands, and at first, she started to pull them away, but his motion was gentle, not threatening. "You have in custody the three men that shot Lavon's bother, Lester."

"Lovester," Abby corrected.

"Your partner knows he has no probable cause, so he is holding them on gun charges and resisting arrest. It's a head game. He knows he must release them soon if I don't leave the shadows and make a deal. He wants me to know letting Dolan know what I did is his best option if it seems to be they getting away with shooting his brother."

"Now you want to make a deal. Well, since you had people try to shoot me, and that did not work, let's hear this deal, and it had better be a real good fucking deal."

Neither seemed to notice they were face to face, almost touching. Abby was surprised at how handsome this man looked close up. She could smell the bittersweet smell of aftershave commingling with the natural beast-like scent of a man.

"First, the shooter will confess to attempted murder. The other two will admit to accessory to commit murder."

Abby's eyes went wide. Damn that Lavon, she thought this was the type of shit he did. Negotiation and knowing when someone was in your head. "So, what do you want for this?"

"First, let me tell you a little story, and it may explain my request. Years and years ago, when I was a small boy, we lived in a small cottage-style home. One of our neighbors had a young man come over and do some plumbing repairs for her. The neighbors knew our house had similar issues, having been built at the same time. The young man inspected the possible work and gave my mother an estimate. My father happened to come home just in time to see the young man going out the back door back to the neighbors as my father was coming in the front door. My father beat my mother in front of me. He wanted me to know that as men, women are our property." Then Malone's eyes turned back, not addressing Abby, she could not help but notice the brilliant grey tent of his eyes now reflected a humanness she had not read about in the file she had read on him. Abby tried not to be drawn into the swell of what he must have gone through to reveal the part of himself. He is the bad guy. He tried to have you killed, she thought to herself, but still, he was trapped like a deer in the headlights and seeing more than a stereotypical villain. She saw a man who wrestled with inner demons, unlike those chasing her one day at a time.

"My mother never looked at me the same from that day forward. She had been depleted of her dignity. And until the day he died, I hated him for what he did to create the relationship void I felt. A relationship holes no woman to this day has stood the chance of filling."

Abby fell back into the cush seating of the limo.

"I want you to promise me that when you arrest Desi, you will try as hard as you can not to kill him. I am aware of your reputation for knowing how to shoot someone you may not have a case against that will stand up in court. I will tell you where to find the rifle he used, but when it comes time for him to appear in court, you and your partner will not contest the plea for mental help for his young man."

"Why?" Abby knew the question hardly sufficed, but she had to start somewhere.

"Because no boy should ever die because he did what he thought he had to in defending his mother and her dignity. I believe he only recently learned the whole story, so even though the crime was old, the pain and scars are fresh for him." Malone sat back and started out the window as if watching a ghost from his past walk along the streets.

"What about the District Attorney's office? We have no control over them?"

"That part has been handled."

Abby knew this meant something illegal had transpired behind the scenes, but she dared not pursue the question. "What is in this for you?"

"I lost over 100 million dollars to those freaks that rob my computer accounts. I am getting 12 percent wherever the new football team ends up."

"The man on the phone when I got in the car was ordering you out of Dolan Dodds territory. And what about the mayor?"

"I am being asked to withdraw. That makes the mayor more you and your partner's problem than mine. Good luck, Abigale."

The limo door opened, and they were right back where they had started, or were they?

"He isn't what I expected," Abby told the footman who helped her from the car.

"None of us are." The footman smiled back.

"I AM NOT SURE WHY I am here, son." The mayor stated. The mayor sat in a conference room in the police station. Mildred Lance sat in a chair facing him. Lavon sat at the head of the table, and Abby stood pacing.

"Please don't call me son; that disrespects my father." Lavon snapped back.

"He is telling you his father isn't a rapist." Abby chimed in, and Mildred's eyes shot toward her.

"You know." Mildred seemed amazed.

"The detective took the original case and stole the original file." Lavon raised the file folder he had in front of him. "It contains pictures, statements, and the DNA samples from the rape kit. You would be surprised of the advances in DNA testing over the last twenty years or so."

The mayor started trying to loosen his tie as if it had suddenly started to choke him. The mayor stood and faced the wall and rested his palms on the wall. "That's why you turned my job offer down. You don't want a share of the pie; you want the whole thing. You and that filthy Dolan,"

"Mr. Mayor, I have been in town a lot longer than my partner, and I can't recall hearing any story about Dolan Dodd raping a poor black secretary and forcing her into servitude. I also never heard where he forced a girl to marry that pencil dick Hardcastle so he could watch his kid grow up. So, you may want to slow down the name calling." Abby was a decibel below screaming.

Lavon and Abby had arrested Desi and recovered the gun he used in the crimes. Abby made sure no one harmed Desi.

"Look, Lavon, there are billions potentially on the table here. A little fuck up in my past shouldn't sink this whole town. And it is not a reason to put it in the hands of organized crime."

"A little fuck up," Mildred screamed. "You raped me both vagally and anally. I was a virgin. It took stitches to fix that little fuck up. When I tried to run, you beat the shit out of me. I still can't sleep with all the lights out." Mildred was now crying. There was more she wanted to say, but she could not form the words.

"Back up those tears, Mildred. You are not totally without fault. You let Malone use your son as a test of faith by having Desi shoot the bodyguard." Abby stated.

"I thought the two of you were working for him when I heard you executed the two men that came for Dolan." Mildred pointed at the mayor.

"Ms. Lance, where should we go with this?" Lavon asked.

The mayor turned around and faced the people in the room again. "I know it doesn't mean anything, Mildred, but I am so sorry. I was a wild frat kid, and I was drunk with no idea how to handle a woman who gave me the urges you did. I confessed to my father, and he put the plan in motion to hide the truth. Go to the press and tell them what you must but give me 12 hours to talk to my wife first. She has been there through sickness and health. And Lavon, I hear you are marrying Lynn; please find a way to tell her that doesn't make her hate me any more than she has to."

"I want to make an offer of restitutions, Detective." Mildred looked at Lavon.

"What do you have in mind?"

"There is no need to destroy any more lives if we can stop this now. First, the mayor pays for Desi's legal defense. Then, he pays for any medical or mental treatment my son needs. And last, he puts him in his will. I don't want anything from you, mayor, but to keep in mind, my baby is a Dodd. Hardcastle's might be slaves, but Dodd's are not."

Chapter 17

When Abby got home, she was prepared for a knockdown drag out with her landlord regarding the busted window and the bullet holes in her apartment. Instead, he was friendly and pleasant. The landlord explained that he had received a visit from what he thinks are mob underworld, and they paid for the repairs and were told that if he gave Abby any grief, they would return and they would not be so pleasant.

Abby now kneeled on the floor, teaching Cletus a new trick. She had bought a bell and put it on the floor, and when she said ring, he would ring the bell, and she would give him a treat. Cletus liked the trick so much he decided to teach Abby a trick. Cletus found the bell after the game. Cletus then laid the bell on the floor and rang it, waiting for Abby to bring his treat.

She did.

Abby scooped Cletus up. "You boys do really love your mommas, don't you." Abby thought about the limo ride with Malone. "Kinda sad when the gangsters treat you better than your fellow cops."

Abby stroked Cletus's head. "I met a man. He is not a good man, and he knows it. But the demons that chase him or a lot like the ones that chase mommy." She smiled at Cletus wide eyes stare. "Don't you worry about your momma. I am going to make it one day at a time."

"I HEARD DETECTIVE O'LEARY is really pissed off at you."
Agent Patterson stated. Agent Patterson and Joan, his wife, were joining Lavon and Lynn for dinner, but they stopped by Patrick's Bar and Grill for a drink first. Lynn rested her head on Lavon while the group enjoyed light drinks and watched Nya destroy Wendell and Webber at darts.

"So, what evil thing did my future husband do now?" Lynn held her head up slightly.

"He solved two of O'Leary's cases, the Dolan attempted murder and the murder of his bodyguard using information that O'Leary should have had." Agent Patterson answered.

"The fiend," Joan commented. Joan and Lynn wore similar dresses they had picked up while shopping and waiting for the guys to get off work.

"Not only that, but the director of the FBI also wants to thank Lavon and Abby for their work this week. They prevented a major mob confrontation and helped to get Donovan Malone out of town. If you allow an organism in a nonindigenous environment, you cannot control its growth. Like those vines someone imported from China, because they thought they would look good on their house over thirty years ago now, they are growing everywhere in this country, and you can't get rid of them."

Joan put her beer down and looked at Lavon. "I stopped by to check on your brother before I left the hospital. He is doing much better, but we want to keep him longer."

"Is Shavon still trying to get in his room?" Lynn asked.

"No, there is a big Indian that seems to be guarding him, and Paden seems to be watching over him. And I think the little lawyer sister of yours has some sort of court order that she cannot be in the room with him without a blood relative."

"Well, it looks like you earned your pay for this week. Young man, the undercover stuff you have been doing could someday backfire on you." Agent Patterson advised. "We don't want you to end up one of those anonymous stars on a wall in D.C."

The conversation had gotten a little too serious for Joan, so she asked. "Where are you two going to honeymoon?"

"I wanted Hawaii," Lavon answered. "Judging from the baby bump on Nya there it's the place to be."

Nya heard the comment and stuck out her tongue at the group.

"I want Lamont, Mississippi," Lynn answered.

"What the hell is there?" Agent Patterson.

"Real people who raise their families with love and values. I want to sit on the back porch and listen to Lavon's mom tell me about the kids growing up. I want to hear Lavon's father do his pathetic Mick Jagger impersonation. I want to hang out with his sisters and play practical jokes with his brothers." They were all watching Lynn now. "I want to be normal for a while."

"Well, Amen," Joan concluded.

Don't miss out!

Visit the website below and you can sign up to receive emails whenever Alex Mitchell publishes a new book. There's no charge and no obligation.

https://books2read.com/r/B-A-UGUAB-HAVQC

BOOKS 2 READ

Connecting independent readers to independent writers.

Also by Alex Mitchell

Welcome to Shepherds Pass
Revenge at Shepherds Pass
Treasure at Shepherds Pass
Welcome to Shepherds Pass
Man Among the Missing
Noreen Tyler
Robinhood at Shepherds Pass
That Which Makes Us Who We Are
Secrets That Bind Family
Balance of Power in Shepherds Pass

www.ingramcontent.com/pod-product-compliance
Lightning Source LLC
Chambersburg PA
CBHW030339020726
47493CB00004B/1333